THE WITCH'S TOWER

Book 1 of the Max Series

David W. Walker

COPYRIGHT

Copyright 2021
David W. Walker

Fanzig House
1904 Evergreen Lane
Hattiesburg, Mississippi 39401
United States

Paperback
Library of Congress Control Number: 2021900206

Version No. 4/13/2021/MST/PB

DEDICATION

I wish to dedicate this work and all stories of *Gaspaar* to those writers who first moved me in my love of children's fantasy and young adult writing and as guides to a richer deeper world behind the illusion of the mundane: C.S. Lewis, Lewis Carroll and Madeleine L'Engle.

Special thanks for long term encouragement, critique, and support from the scholarly brother and sister team of Joseph and Breann Leake, the SCBWI chapter of New Orleans, and my family — especially my mother, Dorothy Walker, who kindled my love of reading as a child and who loved this particular story.

David W. Walker

INTRODUCTION

Dear Reader,

The Tales of Gaspaar are told of a long-forgotten time at the edge of a legend whose retellings have grown wide and wild. Time and tongue have added and lost many of those things we look to set in the world around us. Mountains and rivers and lords and ladies change names and places. Yet the stories live because the dragons and wizards even of our day are only reflections; shadows of something out of all time together. May this telling of such tales inspire those best dreams in the reader and encourage the living of a quest in us all. May you journey with hope no matter the darkness and find light on that way. There are good friends to be found in the strangest places and behind all manner of faces. There is much good...and more.

--your honored scribe--

CHAPTER 1

THE BROTHERS SURPRISED

The royal cook and the queen's maid were talking in the palace kitchen when a breathless page rushed in.

"Have you seen Prince Max? I've been sent to fetch him."

The cook frowned. "Is the prince in more trouble?"

The page caught his breath. "No, no. The King wants to see all his sons in the throne room at once. I think there is going to be an adventure or quest of some sort."

"A *true quest* for Max?" The maid was surprised. "He's just made his thirteenth birthday! He's never had any such thing as that before."

"Good! Good!" The cook laughed. "High time for it then, I say. Max is in the stable. If he's finished shoveling out the stalls. He'll be excited about this."

As the page hurried away from the door the maid started to leave as well. "A quest for Max, *indeed*! What's the king thinking? Wait until I tell the wine steward."

"Now, don't you start gossiping about Max and telling things you don't know about." The cook pointed a flour-coated finger at her. "Mark you, there's always trouble for someone when people don't mind what they say."

As she went her way the maid rolled her eyes at the cook. "*Old worry wart,*" she thought. "*What harm could come from just talking? What's the use in knowing a secret if you can't share it?*"

King Randrew's youngest son stroked the mane of the spotted yearling he was feeding as he rested from his labors. "Nothing exciting ever happens around here, Blueberry. When I'm a knight like Derek I shall make a great journey. Beyond the Lumbadil — maybe to the Runruggle Mountains themselves. We'd see the wide world then, Blue. No one to tell us no, whatever adventure we tried."

The yearling kept eating the oats and did not seem interested in journeys, great or otherwise. She raised her ears at the page's hurried footsteps.

"Prince Max! Your father commands you to the throne room immediately," the page called, drawing up at the stable entrance.

"Rats. What visiting noble are we being shown off to

now, Derwin?" He patted Blueberry and tossed the last of the oats into her trough. He would rather have stayed for chores at the stables even as punishment than be shown to courtly visitors. That was most often the reason he had been called to the throne room before. At least there was no mention of a bath.

"Why can't we begin now?" Prince Gerald fumed. "Max is always late, and I am missing a game of chess with the court jester. Besides, Max is too young for serious talk, if that is indeed what it is to be."

"Oh, let it go, Gerald," Prince Derek said. He was tired of waiting too but couldn't stand to hear his brother complain. "I think Max is worth a bit more than a silly game of chess."

"It is only silly to you, Derek," Gerald goaded, "because you can never win."

"Boys . . . boys!" The King could not bear to hear them argue. Would even his most loyal subjects hope for a worthy heir to the throne if they should hear the quarreling of his sons? Randrew longed for the quiet of the moat where he had spent the morning seeking an answer to the great question that had fallen upon him now.

Arriving at the chamber door, Max brushed loose straw off his tunic before entering, hoping he'd wiped his boots clean enough as well. Stepping inside, he saw there were no guests or servants, only his father and his brothers, yet the king seemed solemn as he sat upon the throne and his brothers looked uneasy. It must be very important, he thought. Something serious.

"Here he is then," Gerald sighed. "Can we begin at last?"

Derek motioned for Max to stand beside him and Gerald.

When all the brothers were quiet, the king rose and

taking his walking staff moved to stand looking at each of his sons in turn. Max wondered at this, for it was not his father's way. In the long moment before the king spoke Max began to sense a concern in his father's presence that he had not known before. The crease above the king's brows was deep as he looked them over. It wasn't like his father to hold back in such silence. When he spoke, his next words seemed more like a speech than talk among the family.

"My sons, it has come to pass, that I must choose very soon the heir to my throne . . . the crown of Gaspaar."

Randrew saw that each son was much surprised at the words he spoke as he had known they would be.

Max had grown up knowing that such a day must some time come, but surely not *now*. His father was not so old as that! The idea that he and his older brothers would be judged now for such a choice was hard to imagine. This was the most serious thing he had ever heard.

Only Gerald was quick to speak. "Please, Father, whom have you chosen?"

The King took a measured breath before he continued in this formal way of speaking, "To be a king is not only a high honor but more, it is a great responsibility. On his decisions, lives may be changed for good or for bad. Plenty and famine each challenge him. He must always consider the needs of his people and the actions which may bring great risk that others do not see. It is a hard duty. It is a high role, but it is a servant's role. After much thought and pondering, I have decided upon a test which will determine the most able and worthy of you to be the future king."

Max's mouth was dry.

King Randrew cleared his throat before continuing. "I am sending you all on a trial or quest. Each of you shall have a horse and a small bag of gold to carry with you. You are to find the greatest treasure in all the land. On the last day of May, you must return to the palace courtyard. There your treasures will be judged. The son who has brought back the greatest treasure; he will be the future king. You shall leave tomorrow. Go and prepare now, my sons. Do not speak of this beyond our family."

Max was so surprised at his father's words that he could say nothing. He did not know what he should do next. He followed his brothers without speaking.

As they left the chamber, Gerald made a sign for the others to follow him into a side room off the hall. Gerald quietly closed the door behind them. Turning to Derek and Max he smiled in a way that Max did not like.

"Well, my brothers, it seems we are in for a great adventure. I would imagine it will be more than enough of a true test of a future king. Yet, I fear it is perhaps too great a danger to be taken by us all. We might not all return, if you understand me."

Max felt a flicker of worry at Gerald's words, but a growing excitement at the idea of a quest of his own — something he'd only dreamed of until this day.

Derek frowned. "Speak plainly, Gerald."

Gerald put a hand on Max's shoulder. "Derek, it is all very well for you and me to risk our lives in this venture. After all, we are both older and have had other travels and know our way about the lands. But Max has never had such experiences. Truthfully, I am worried for his life. I feel we should make sure, before all else, that he is safe."

"What do you mean?" Derek asked.

"We might take Max to stay with some friends of mine beyond the river until this test is over. He could tell Father any tales he wished or imagined, and we could provide him some reasonable treasure to return with. I would not have him embarrassed, of course."

Max felt his face grow hot with anger. "That would be a lie! It's true I've had no great adventures like either of you — but if this is my chance — I mean to try my own."

Derek nodded. "I wasn't much older than Max when I first rode as a squire to Sir Claire. I don't think it is up to us what Max does, Gerald. If Father says he's ready, that's enough. Besides, it will teach him a thing or two if he will keep his head."

Gerald's eyes narrowed. "Don't forget I warned you — both of you."

Max turned to his oldest brother when Gerald stormed from the room. "I mean to try this thing, Derek. I wish Gerald wouldn't always treat me like such a child. "

Derek looked at the door Gerald had slammed behind him. "Gerald is not like he used to be. Sometimes he cheats at cards and dice I think." He paused. "I wonder if he is trying to cheat at this?"

Max shook his head. "Well, if there are no rules to an adventure, I guess you can't cheat."

"There are always rules, Brother. A knight carries them with him, even when he's alone."

Derek had often taken Max camping over the summers, treating him as a young squire, but Max knew a true quest like this was quite a different matter. His oldest brother reminded him of many things about traveling on the roads that evening; how to keep a tinder box dry when crossing a flooded stream, that moss grows most on the northward side of trees and, after again practicing his sword-play, cautioned him to keep the blade clean. He reminded Max that, next to caring for his horse, the cleanliness of his sword was the sign of a proper knight.

Settling finally to bed, Max feared he would not sleep at all. He was glad when Queen Maeve stopped to visit his bedchamber as the palace darkened for the night. His mother sat on the side of his mattress and taking his hand, held it in her lap.

"Your hands have grown large. I remember when I could hold them both in one palm. Pink as a primrose and soft as a mouse's ear. Now here are these long fingers browned with sun, scrapes from chores, and scars from your practice with Derek's old sword." She shook her head.

"I've grown up, Mother."

"We are always growing up, my Max. I know. And I am glad you relish this quest with such joy. But are you not even a little bit afraid?"

"I don't think so. Not much." Max looked at his mother. "Are you?"

Queen Maeve patted his hand. "No more than I think I must be." She sighed. "I shall not plead for you to be always careful, but I ask you to be . . . mindful. You are a brave boy and you have my heart, as do your brothers though they are not my own blood." She paused. "I am not so worried at which of you shall be chosen king as I am of what men you shall become. You will change on this journey, my son. Each day will bring a new world. Remember my prayers are with you all. Stay true to what matters, for that may look different from a far place or a dark passage. It is what you choose to follow that will make your path clear."

Max was not so sure at the queen's words, but he knew her heart. "Don't worry, Mother, I will be —," he caught himself, "mindful."

Remembering Max's many childhood mischiefs, scrapes, and foolish stunts, Maeve raised his hand to kiss and rose to leave her youngest son to his dreams. It seemed so soon to put him to such a test, she thought, but Randrew himself had been given little choice and life must be faced as it came and not as one wished.

CHAPTER 2

THE QUEST BEGINS

Max was surprised when the morning rooster crowed in the courtyard. It seemed no time had passed from his having blown out his candle. For just a moment he did not remember why he was so excited. Then, seeing his pack, sword, and traveling clothes laid out, everything came back in a flash. The great quest waited. His quest.

The prince bounded out of bed and into his leather britches. Hopping around the room, first on one foot and then the other, he tugged on his favorite deerskin hunting boots. He was still pulling on his shirt as he bounced across the hall to a small private chamber at the corner of the castle. Here he paused to sit on the cold smooth stones with the round opening that dropped away to darkness. After a few moments he reached for the small rags that the maid had laid out on the ledge by the single window. He knew he would likely be using leaves for this purpose in the weeks ahead. He would miss the luxuries of the castle. An adventure would mean changes in all manner of ways.

Reaching the kitchen Max found the cook had prepared not only his breakfast but, at the queen's request, had also stocked a road pack with dried foods that would last many days if he were prudent. Though the queen had not mentioned the purpose of the pack, the cook had assumed this command must pertain to the rumored quest he and the queen's maid had discussed when the page had come searching for the prince.

The cook was not alone in his thinking for when Queen Maeve had come to the kitchen the previous evening the queen's maid had followed her lady. She listened at the keyhole as she sometimes did and rushed to tell the wine steward all she had learned or suspected, who of course promised he would speak no further of it — as he always did. Not once did she think of the cook's warning about trouble that comes when people don't mind what they say.

This morning in the stable, Max's brothers were already saddling their horses. Gerald wore a fine green cloak with a bright yellow jacket underneath. Topping it off, he sported a velvet cap, with a long red feather. His horse, Gonrest, was the most valuable steed in the stable, a present on his eighteenth birthday. But it was not Gerald's finery that made Max stare.

Derek was wearing his shirt of mail. The armor was formed from hundreds of little metal rings joined like links of chain. Over this polished metal armor, Derek wore a scarlet cape with a golden lion of Gaspaar sewn on it. He could see that Derek's sword, shield, and helmet were strapped to the saddle of his great yellow charger, Moonstone, who he had been given on his knighting a year ago at nineteen years of age. Looking at Derek made Max want to be off on the roadway. His oldest brother looked like an adventure.

Derek pointed across the stable and Max turned to see Blueberry eyeing his saddle which waited on a wooden rail beside a bridle. "You must think first of your horse, Max. Be sure to see that she has fed before you worry about your own stomach. Remember to comb her down when she has ridden hard for you. Do this and she will take you a long way and do it happily. Now, set your saddle and settle your pack. The king is to see us in the courtyard in a moment."

Gerald looked over his mount as he led Gonrest out of the stable. "There is a lot of hard work in a quest, and Derek and I will not be there to help you. There is still time for you to stay with my friends."

Max gave Gerald an angry glance as he heaved his saddle over the blanket he had settled on Blueberry's back.

Later, as the brothers rode away from the castle and out of the town, Max remembered the king's parting words and warning; "There are many enemies among the far lands, my sons. If some giant or witch knew you traveled near, they would make great plans to catch you or worse. Trust only those who may be trusted."

At first the princes talked a great deal about where they should go. Southward toward Umber and Camelot was too well-ridden to offer much hope of unknown treasures Derek maintained, and Gerald had little use for the westward lands of Averon or Wotterham which had grown cold to Gaspaar's friendship in recent years. They determined that they should travel to the inn on the Lumbadil River, where the northeastern frontier began. They might go their separate ways the next morning. "All true adventures start beyond the river," Derek said.

Max was glad they would stay together at least until he got used to long riding, finding the rhythm that worked best between rider and horse. By late afternoon he was tired and sore but did not complain. He knew if he did, Gerald would insist that he go to stay with his friends.

Finally, when the sun was casting long shadows in front of them, they heard a rushing sound that grew clearer as they rode. Topping a rise in the roadway, Max could see the Lumbadil ran before them. Its cool waters splashed and gurgled around gray stone supports of the ancient bridge. Max had not seen the river since childhood and never crossed to the fabled frontier beyond its banks. It seemed both strange and familiar at the same time, as if he were recalling it from a distant dream. He was so fascinated he almost forgot how tired and hungry he had become. The windows of the inn glowed warmly on the far bank, and Max remembered that this was the last boundary of the land he knew. He wondered what waited for him in the growing dark beyond those lights.

CHAPTER 3

AT THE RED LION INN

The Red Lion was a crude but pleasant inn, popular with travelers of high and low station in those days. The stables were clean, and the princes saw that their horses would be well cared for. The innkeeper was happy to have three new guests for the night and promised their rooms would be comfortable with fresh straw bedding. The brothers had decided among themselves not to use their titles in order to avoid drawing unwelcome attention here.

Max was hungry for supper, but Derek said he should have a bath first, as after a day on horse, it was good manners to the other diners. Besides, it was likely to be his last bath for some time. He agreed, though he did not care to, and found that the bath was cold, unlike the heated ones at the castle. He was so tired that it felt good anyway and enjoyed his supper more because of it.

The three brothers sat at a table near the large stone fireplace to be served. Derek laughed when Max grabbed his water cup after taking his first bite of the steaming shepherd's pie. "You'll wish you had food that hot before a week is out," he chuckled.

The food was plain fare, but well cooked, which Derek said was most often true of the Lion's table. Pushing away their empty plates, the brothers listened to the tales other guests were telling to entertain each other. It was fun hearing the stories, but they also listened for any hint of treasure that might be mentioned. Some of the yarns were rather long and fanciful. An old tinker was explaining how in his youth he had tricked his wife into believing he was a prince in disguise. It was an amusing tale, though Max wondered what the man might say if he knew three true princes listened to him now.

He was just nodding off when the tinker stopped in the middle of a word. This startled Max and he jerked his head up to find everyone staring behind him. Curious, he followed their gaze and found a most striking and unusual pair of travelers had entered the room.

Just inside the doorway stood a tall and majestic lady to whom all eyes were drawn. Beneath her black road cape, she wore a rich purple dress and long white gloves with jeweled fingers. Her eyes were greener than the deep forest and glistened beneath dark lashes. Braided, fiery-copper hair, showed at the edges of a white silken wimple framing her snowy cheeks and brow. It was obvious she was a noblewoman by both her dress and confident manner. Max hardly knew what to make of her and felt a sudden awkwardness as her gaze met his own. The other figure was a hard-wrinkled little man with heavy-browed eyes and a fierce look to his narrow, squinty, face. There was no question of it, he was the first mountain dwarf that the prince had ever seen for himself.

"Make way for the Duchess!" the dwarf commanded sharply and pushed Max aside as the prince had attempted to rise from his seat in courtly respect. This took Max by such surprise that he tripped over his chair and fell sprawling on his back. Before he could rise, Max was aware of several things happening at once; Derek grabbed the dwarf up by his arms and while the angry little man struggled cursing in his brother's grip, the noblewoman knelt to touch Max's cheek with concern, yet before he could even answer her query, Gerald was at the lady's side apologizing for his young brother's clumsiness.

All these things happened almost in one moment and Max only knew that he was glad Derek was beside him with this fantastic "Duchess" so close above him. Her gloved hand had felt cold against his cheek and the concern in her dark eyes had seemed to stare into him in a strange way.

After everyone apologized — the Duchess had made the dwarf apologize too — Derek and Gerald insisted that she join their table. Since the brothers offered no more than their first names, it seemed impolite to inquire more of the lady than her title. Nobles often traveled in secret and did not wish to reveal their full names for any number of reasons. The brothers, not wishing to share their relationship to the King of Gaspaar, naturally respected her similar anonymity. From here on, the lady was referred to only as "Duchess." Indeed, from that day forth, the brothers would always think first of *her* when anyone announced the presence of any lady of that same title.

Derek and Gerald talked while the lady was served her supper. It was clear that both were much attracted to her.

Derek told stories about fighting ogres and saving young maidens. Max was bemused and embarrassed at the way his oldest brother dressed up some of his adventures. They had never sounded quite so gallant before.

Gerald could hardly wait his turn. He told clever tales and jokes. Most of the funny — and foolish — stories were about his brothers. Gerald had an amazing memory for mistakes and mischief Max had gotten into that he had rather hoped were forgotten.

The Duchess showed delight with every word the brothers spoke, and Max wondered how anyone could bear hearing them brag so on themselves. Soon they were all laughing at even the silliest things. The young prince felt uncomfortable. He did not like laughing at jokes that were not really funny and was not enjoying himself at all. He noticed that the dwarf, who had not spoken since his apology, was not laughing either. The little man sat back puffing a foul-smelling pipe, watching the others through a twisting cloud of smoke.

Max excused himself and made his way upstairs to bed. He wanted to be rested for an early start in the morning.

It was still dark night when Max woke. Derek sat at the edge of his bed shaking his arm. He saw by a small candle that his oldest brother was dressed for travel.

Derek whispered. "I'm sorry to wake you, Max, but I wanted you to know I am leaving."

"What?" Max pushed up from his pillow.

Derek put a finger to his lips to quiet him. "The Duchess knows all kinds of things. It is surely good fortune that let us meet her. She has told me where a great treasure is. It lies far to the northwest of here and there will be much danger. Dragons and magic wait for me, and there is so far to go that I should leave tonight."

Max knew that Derek must indeed go but felt sad. He would have liked to share Derek's journey, but knew he must find his own treasure.

Derek shook his hand. "Be careful not to tell Gerald where I'm headed. He might have ideas about sneaking along."

Max was sorry his oldest brother did not trust Gerald but thought he might indeed be wise not to. "Be careful, Derek," he said.

"Of course!" Derek almost laughed but caught himself and, taking the small candle holder with him, slipped out the doorway. He had his own kind of adventure before him, and he was set to enjoy it.

Morning came and Max wondered what Gerald would do when he found Derek gone. He need not have worried for he discovered Gerald had also disappeared in the night as well. Max asked the innkeeper if he knew of this. The man could only say that he had seen him talking with the noble lady until very late and not since. Max wondered what he should do next when a cool gloved hand touched his shoulder. He whirled to find the Duchess smiling at him.

"Would you have breakfast with me?" she asked.

Max thought to say no, but something about her eyes and the hand on his shoulder made it easier to say yes. Despite his first misgivings, Max found the Duchess full of cheerful talk and soon began to relax and enjoy his breakfast as she recounted the night's conversation after the youngest brother had left the party.

". . . Of course, both your brothers were so excited and anxious to be off on their quests. I implored them to wait on a good night's rest before they began their journeys, but it seems they have deserted us both for all my pleas. For such strapping lords, they do behave as boys even yet." As she laughed, Max laughed with her, agreeing with her judgment of his brothers' natures, and it just seemed natural to share the lady's mirth. Perhaps he had misjudged her.

The Duchess shook a tear of laughter from her eye with a gloved finger. "You see, I did indeed know of three such treasures as they sought. As to which they should choose to pursue, I could not say. Only the stars know which is greatest."

Max wondered how this lady knew of such fortunes to begin with, but he never quite asked her. It was hard to say anything while the Duchess talked. She spoke with great delight and described things so that they almost appeared before his eyes.

"What of the third treasure, my Lady?" Max asked. "The one that neither Derek nor Gerald chose to seek?"

The Duchess smiled. Looking first over each of her shoulders she leaned very close to Max to speak in a secretive whisper.

"There is a land far to the east where grow flowers of solid gold. The grass is silver, and the water is wine. At the very center of that forest is a small tree of great beauty. Its color is so beautiful it has no name. You, my brave young Prince, should dig it up and bring it to your royal father."

Max was surprised that she seemed to know who his father was. "For what purpose would I pull up such a tree? What good would come of it? Would it not die?"

The lady smiled and her teeth gleamed. "Ahhhh, but

this small tree is *magic*. Why, you could plant it in your father's garden. All the palace grounds would be turned to beauty and light." She began to sing a strange chant, almost a song, so quietly that Max could barely hear it, and yet he could hear nothing else. Nothing else mattered. The adventure was calling to him.

"On the road, through forest old,
the way will open for the bold.
The flowers are gold, the grasses silver,
wine rushes down the banks of the river.

"Deep inside, at the heart of the splendor,
a tree grows now, bright beyond color.
The brave alone may pluck that root,
and bring back the magic chute.

"Treasure without measure lies unclaimed.
The bold adventurer calls it game.
Let no beast or burden stand in your way;
Many would try to turn you astray.

"Nothing is greater than its glory.
Hurry east, or forever, be sorry."

When she had finished, the Duchess warned Max to speak to no one of his journey. She handed him a small map, telling him to carry it hidden in his boot.

The prince was grateful, but one thing bothered him as the noblewoman left the inn that morning. Her servant smiled at him. It was not a pretty smile. Though the dwarf's thin lips drew upward at the corners, his hard, little eyes showed no flicker of friendship. That cold look would stay with Max as he

remembered their parting. There are smiles, and there are
smiles.

CHAPTER 4

AN UNHAPPY CHOICE

Max went around to the stable that morning after loading his pack and Blueberry whinnied to greet him. "We have a true adventure ahead of us now, girl," he replied as he patted her spotted brown muzzle. He was fitting her bridle when he heard strange noises outside. A small woolly head poked inside the stable door and bleated. Outside, a large flock of sheep swarmed around the inn complaining in their shrill, overlapping, voices. Among them a great black dog barked and scratched at the entrance of the inn. Spying the prince, the dog dropped back from the door and ran toward him.

Max was nervous, for the dog was large and very excited. He grasped the handle of his sword but stood still and tried not to show fear. The big dog stopped just before him and whined. It then turned and ran away a short distance but stopped again to bark back at him. Relieved, Max was curious at this odd behavior. Then — the strangest thing of all the strange things that had happened since his arrival at the inn — the dog *called* to him.

"Follow!"

The prince was stunned. Had he truly heard what he thought he had heard? Had the animal really spoken? He shouted after the running dog. "Wait! Wait! Did you speak?" But the dog was halfway across the bridge before Max mounted Blueberry and charged after it.

As he rode, he wondered again if he had imagined the spoken word. "*Follow* — it *must* be a dream," he said, but seeing the dog glancing back at him again and again as it ran on, he thought, *surely it wants me to follow*.

After they had traveled back over the road toward Gaspaar almost a mile, the dog rushed to a stop beneath a large oak. Max saw a dark shape lying on the ground in the shadow of the tree. Riding closer he could see that it was a man. Probably the shepherd of the dog's distressed flock, he imagined.

Max could tell the dog's master was very sick for he was groaning and rolling his head from side to side. When Max touched his hand to the shepherd's forehead it felt like a boiling pot. He wished he had Derek there to help him but looking at the poor dog sitting beside the shepherd, he knew he must do something. "Well, sir dog," he said, "I wish you could give me a hand, but I guess this is what an adventure means — troubles with no help." He struggled, dragging the poor old man to his feet, and leaned him against Blueberry's side. Pushing and pulling the moaning shepherd across the saddle was harder still. Even though the man was quite frail and thin, Max was out of breath when he finally started back up the road to the inn.

The large dog trotted beside him. It made no noise but sometimes pressed its pointy black nose against the shepherd's hands which hung down the horse's side. Just before they came to the river bridge again, the dog ran ahead to the inn.

By the time Max and Blueberry crossed the bridge, the innkeeper Joel and his wife Maude were hurrying out to meet them.

"Why it's old Dimbarrel!" Maude exclaimed. "What has happened?"

The innkeeper touched the shepherd's forehead. "It seems he has taken a fever, Maude." He turned to Max. "You are a good lad to bring him to us, young sir."

They carried the sick man into the inn where a bed was made ready. There were no other guests staying over that morning, so they took him to the best room.

"Will he be all right?" Max asked.

"Well now, it's hard to tell," Joel said. "He will have to stay in bed for a time, that is certain." When he said this, the shepherd stirred and tried to talk. They leaned closer to hear. After a minute the innkeeper nodded and stood back up. "He's asleep now, but he must have heard what I said about staying here for a while."

"What did he say?" Max asked.

Joel motioned for the prince to follow him out of the room as the shepherd fell back into his fevered sleep.

"Now the problem is this, young sir. Dimbarrel in there has his whole flock of sheep headed home from the market and nowhere to keep them except at his farm up in the

Runruggel Mountains. The grass around here's a bit too thin and people don't like feeding another man's flock for free."

"Can't he send for someone to take them home for him?"

The innkeeper shook his head. "I'm afraid not. He lives alone and his only kin is quite far from here. It'll be a fortnight or more before I could even hope to get one of his nephews down here. He can't afford to pay anyone. I'd go but I have the inn. Besides, there's no one 'round about here that wouldn't just as soon steal that old man's sheep as tend them."

Max was upset. "It looks like I have not helped the shepherd much after all. He will live, but all he has will be lost." Something Max didn't want to think about was nagging at him. Someone was still needed to help the old shepherd. Well, hadn't he done something already? And hadn't the Duchess that very morning warned him about letting no burden stand in the way of his treasure? Her soft, rhyming, whisper-song came into his mind so clear that, for just one moment, he thought he must hurry for the road east and all it promised, or he would worry forever at its loss.

But there was something else. *"There are always rules, brother. A knight carries them with him, even when he's alone."* It had sounded so right at home when he had imagined setting off on a great quest. Now with his real adventure calling him, it sounded different. A voice seemed to ask if it were still true. Wasn't this a special situation? Max considered how his brothers might answer that question. He knew what his own answer would be, though he did not like it.

"That is it then," the prince said, "I'll take the shepherd's flock to the mountains." As he said it, he knew he was going out of the way of his treasure already. If it was the right thing to do, he wondered why he did not feel better about it.

CHAPTER 5

DANGER IN THE NIGHT

After packing for the journey Max returned to the shepherd's room. Max leaned in close to hear the old man's ragged whisper. "You're a brave lad," Dimbarrel said and stopped to take a deep breath. "Those who . . . do good deeds . . ." he could not finish the thought.

Max nodded. "I will try my best, sir," he promised.

The shepherd closed his eyes, but after taking another breath, croaked again in a painful voice. "My dog, Knipper . .

. will guide . . . look after . . . strays . . . watch . . . danger." He strained to say more but only mumbled and fell again into a fitful sleep.

Max tip-toed out of the room and paid the innkeeper for his lodging.

"That is a fine bag of coins you have there," Joel said. "Be careful not to show them much. Some folks would rob you blind. The road's not the place to travel pretty now-a-days."

Max bid goodbye to his hosts and went to saddle Blueberry. The pony was sniffing at the lambs which were playing about her hooves. The shepherd's dog trotted up to him and stood still. It seemed to be waiting for the prince to speak.

"Knipper, you are to be my guide to the mountains," Max said. "Let's go quickly. I have an adventure waiting when our trip is over." He knew his brothers would be far on the way to their treasures. He could well imagine what Gerald would say if he could see him now.

Though the sheep dog had not uttered another word, real or imagined, "Knipper" seemed to understand and rounded up the flock in very fast order. When Max had mounted Blueberry, they were ready to go.

"All right," The prince nodded, "to the Runruggel Mountains, then," and Knipper led them away from the inn.

Max, Blueberry, the sheep and the large black dog, all moved along the road for several hours that morning. Knipper seemed so much in charge of the flock that Max began to wonder what good he was to follow on his horse. As they traveled, his mind wandered. He thought of the Duchess' warning to let nothing turn him away from his treasure. Yet, here he was, already going the wrong direction and doing nothing really important, as far as he could tell. The lady would count him the silliest of the brothers if ever she knew of his journey.

The trip was easy enough and the scenery soon cheered his spirit. The wide road wound around green gentle rises and through plush meadows yellow with summer flowers. Above him the sky was as blue as May skies can be and Max began to enjoy himself. He even tried whistling a song or two as he rode. This helped keep his mind off being hungry for a while as well.

As the sun began to set, he realized he should hunt a place to camp for the night. He was relieved to find a large meadow with a shallow stream running along its bottom. The first stars were appearing as the prince finished gathering wood and began to kindle the campfire.

Max was watching Blueberry, free of her saddle, rolling on her back, when he heard Knipper's bark. It was sharp and fierce and rose over the high voices of excited sheep. He dropped his supper bread and grabbed his sword. Before he had time to be afraid, Max was running toward the loud noises as fast as he could. The night air whistled in his ears.

Nearing the spot where Knipper snapped and barked, he heard a deep voice yelling curses. A large, bearded man with a wide brimmed hat and long gray cloak stood by the creek swinging a heavy staff at the dog and gripping a frightened lamb under his other arm.

"Stop there, Mister!" Max shouted. "Let go that sheep!" He didn't know how he could say such brave words, for he felt himself becoming scared even as he said them.

There was silence and then the man roared with hard laughter when he saw who challenged him. "Well! This is a bit of luck! Are you the shepherd's boy?"

Max swallowed hard as he saw the dagger in the man's belt. "I am the shepherd's man." He turned red as the man laughed at his reply.

"Well, *man*, meet my stick! It should be enough of a switch for you!" The robber swung the long staff toward Max.

Without thinking, Max shifted backwards and parried away the staff. It was just as Derek had taught him. Now he found that all the practice was much more important than the game it had seemed. Blow after blow the man struck at Max. Again, and again he parried the blows away with a two-handed grip. He was almost too frightened to think, but his sword did not seem to know it.

With each swing of the robber's staff, Knipper dashed in to bite at the man's legs. The thief grew madder and madder. With a quick change of his stance, he swung the staff at the dog, striking it hard behind the ears. Knipper fell stunned and the robber threw down his staff and dropped the lamb, pulling a dagger to finish   the dog. At that unguarded moment Max rushed forward. His sword struck the man's hand, making him drop his blade.

The robber screamed and grasped his bleeding wound. As Max raised his sword again, the man ran from the meadow swearing over his shoulder. "We'll get you, lad! We'll get you and all your ruddy sheep! See if we don't!"

Max stood there watching as the robber vanished over the hillside. The excitement that had burned like a fire in his chest left him. Now he felt weak and very small. The prince slumped down next to the dog which lay panting on its side. Everything was so quiet that the fighting seemed like a wild dream. Max almost wondered if it had really happened at all.

Then the dog rolled over and sat up. "Thank you," it said.

Max flinched in disbelief. "I must be dreaming." He pinched himself to make certain. "Ouch!" The pain was real enough. Rising to his knees, he never took his eyes off the dog. "Then you *can* talk. I did hear you at the inn." He might have been afraid, if he had not just had such a terrible fight.

The dog cocked its head sideways and seemed to grin. "As a matter of fact, I do speak, but not often, and not around most people." Knipper waited a moment and then continued. "I owe you my life, young Master. I offer you my friendship and share my secret."

Max felt excited talking to this remarkable creature and a little embarrassed. He could never pet a dog like this one, he decided.

"You are the only talking dog I have ever seen." He was sorry as soon as he said it. It sounded all wrong, like he meant the dog seemed funny or odd.

Before Max could say anything else, Knipper gave a bark that sounded like a laugh. "Perhaps I am. At least the first that ever spoke to you. But I am not the only speaking beast. There are others. They aren't all dogs either."

"Then do all the animals speak?" Max wondered about his puppy at home. He felt ashamed, remembering pulling its tail.

"There were never many of us, I'm afraid," Knipper answered. "There are no speaking beasts in the city, I'm sure. It's not just being able to speak, you know. It's — well, it's like being awake. There are fewer of us awake now and mostly it's wild ones in the woods." The dog sniffed the air. "I believe your supper is burning."

Max hardly cared. There were so many things he wanted to ask. "But why aren't all the animals awake like you?" he asked.

"That is a long story, my young friend, and not told quickly. Perhaps I shall tell it to you at some other time." Knipper blinked his deep brown eyes and let his long pink tongue roll out in a yawn. "Besides, I am quite tired, and we have a way to go on our journey."

Max cleaned his sword as Derek had taught him to and lay on his blanket near the fire. He was so excited that even being as tired as he was, it took him a long time to fall asleep.

CHAPTER 6

DIFFERENT PATHS

It was morning and Max woke to Knipper's barking at the sleepy sheep. As he lay there he wondered if it had all been just a dream. Surely it must have been, he thought, but he heard the dog's voice calling his name and the unbelievable truth came back to him.

"Wake up, young Max. It is time to be going."

He washed his face in the meadow stream. The morning sun was as red as a ripe cherry and climbing out of the trees in the east. Max felt fresh and well rested as he packed his bedroll and whistled for Blueberry. He plucked two apples from a tree near the stream and climbed onto the pony's back. "How far must we travel today, Knipper?" he asked as the dog loped up.

"As far as the wooden bridge over the Willtil River. That is where we leave the flat land and circle 'round the great hills of Gumbor." The dog looked up at the boy. "Are you ready for the ride?"

Max did not want to admit that he didn't know how far it was to the Willtil. "Of course, but you must lead the way."

"*Of course*," Knipper replied with a grin and trotted off to the sheep.

After many hours of following the road, Max noticed that the hills were becoming steeper. The woods were crowding closer and deeper. Except when they were on the top of hills, Max could not see any distance ahead. If this was flat land, he thought, then the hills of Gumbor must be something indeed. The sun was sinking low when Knipper came back to Max in his usual effortless lope.

"There are robbers waiting for us at the bridge," the dog said.

How do you know that?" Max asked, swallowing as sudden fear gripped his chest. "Is the bridge just ahead of us?"

"No, it is some way from here, but a good friend has told me."

Max looked around. "I haven't seen anyone."

Knipper scratched an ear. "Foxes are not often seen when they don't wish to be." He turned and barked to the woods at their right.

After a moment Max saw a beautiful red fox trotting out of the trees. It came toward them with no hint of fear. Knipper turned back to Max. "Master Max, meet Fanzig, the great red fox of Dumwillow Forest."

Max had met kings and queens before. He could never recall meeting anyone who seemed more the noble lord of a kingdom.

The fox, which was smaller than Knipper, looked at Max with twinkling amber eyes and grinned as only a fox can grin. "I hear I have you to thank for saving old Knipper here."

Max fumbled for words to speak. He knew he was seeing something grander than he had ever seen before. He almost forgot that he was himself a prince. "Well, I did what I could."

"Ah, is that not the most any of us may do? The speaking beasts owe you thanks and I shall give it. I come to warn you of the robbers that wait for you at the river bridge. I know another way across the Willtil and would gladly lead you, but there are other dangers."

"What are they?" Max asked.

"First, it is a longer way and may cost you some days," the fox began. "The great problem is that you must cross the hills of Gumbor to reach the Runruggel Mountains from there."

"What of these hills of Gumbor?" Max asked. "Are they so hard to journey through?"

The fox blinked before he replied. "They are said to be home to giants."

Max felt his throat tighten and looked to Knipper. "Do you know about these giants?" He did not like the way his own voice sounded to him when he said the word *giants*.

Knipper sat down. "I have never seen one. I have never met anyone who has. But then, no one goes to the hills of

Gumbor either."

Max turned back to Fanzig. "Have you seen these giants?"

"No," the fox replied, "but none will build a road through the hills. It is unknown to me."

Max thought hard. "These robbers at the bridge, were they many?"

"A dozen perhaps," Fanzig said.

Max chewed his lip. "Then we must travel to Gumbor," he said. "There may, or may not, be giants there, but there are most surely robbers at the bridge. We have no choice."

Knipper looked up at Max. "Except to turn back. Dimbarrel would not ask you to go to Gumbor."

Max almost said yes but did not. Somehow, he felt that to turn back here would be to turn back always. "I have given the shepherd my word, and he has given me his trust. I wish to keep both." Derek would like that, he thought to himself. And Gerald would think him a silly fool. Still, he could not go by what others would think or it would not be his adventure at all, he decided. He had waited too long to waste it now.

***

Derek

Riding the north-most branch of the highroad, Prince Derek admitted he missed Max's company. He had hoped to share a bit more of this adventure with his youngest brother before they must part ways. Still, he considered it a happy fate that let him break free of Gerald and set after a treasure of his own. He thought again of the night at the Red Lion where they had first met the wondrous Duchess.

It had been a jolly evening with plenty of food, drink, and conversation. Though Gerald and Max were both tired of his stories, the Duchess was far more appreciative. Instead of rolling her eyes as he told of the adventures, she had laughed and gasped in all the right places. It was certain that the noble lady truly understood the challenges a knight faced.

As he rode, Derek thought on the story the Duchess had revealed to him apart from the others. Max had long gone to bed, and Gerald had gone to collect a book of olden poetry from his pack to read to them. While he was away, she had leaned closer to Derek. In the flickering light of the table candle she told the tale of treasure that set him on this path. He knew the Duchess had sensed the jealousy of Gerald, and that this quest was too difficult for Max. When she whispered, it was of her confidence in Derek's prowess as a true knight.

"Many pride themselves as knights," she said. "They ride fine horses and bear polished shields. It is glorious to meet, at last, one with the spirit of true chivalry and courage so needed in this dark world. It is for one such as you that I hold a quest that may give both honor and treasure to meet your heart's desire. Yet, while treasure in plenty is indeed waiting, many lives are at stake also."

Derek's heart swelled with pride and excitement. "Pray tell me of this challenge, dear lady," he pleaded.

The Duchess sighed. "In the far land of Empt, on the northwest reaches, at the forest of Quist, lies the woefully cursed village of Kurn. That sad fief has lived beneath the threat of a dragon's bargain for long years. Only days ago, did they suffer the rage of the greatest of the northern dragons; Gorackle. The Earl of Kurn begged for aid, but the king of Empt merely offered a small reward to any who would bring the dragon's head to his court. It is hardly enough to bestir many to such danger." The Duchess shook her head and leaned closer. "But there is more. The dragon has forced many bargains in its long and evil reign. He who slays

Gorackle will have all its ransoms collected through the years."

Now, riding, Derek slipped his hand into his tunic and pulled out a pendant that the lady had given him. It was an old tooth, perhaps two inches long, and tied with a twine thong that held it around his neck. The lady had given him this trinket in secret from the others. "Here," she had whispered, "is the baby tooth of that dragon, Gorackle, that pillages the poor Kurnsmen. Wear it against your bare chest and you shall know when he is near. His hot breath will heat the tooth though it was taken from him long years ago."

Derek had frowned. "It looks like a human tooth to me, though it is clearly no child's."

"A dragon baby is much like a human in the back teeth, my Prince. When this tooth burns against your skin, you shall know that Gorackle kindles his inner fire. You will know he is near at hand. Perhaps you know that a dragon's belly is its weakness? If you should sneak within its cave while it sleeps, the hideous villain will lay unguarded to your sword."

Derek grunted. "I prefer to meet evil in the open. I need room to handle my lance and swing my blade. Twisting about in a dark cave seems more to the liking of the great worms themselves."

"Bold knights often make that mistake. It is courage to fight in-close that will deliver this foul beast to you, Prince Derek. Grand moves on a field of fair play will leave you brave and dead. It takes courage rare to go into the very den of the enemy. And you will have the one warning of his presence. The chance in a hundred will be yours, or perhaps you would discard my *one* true gift to you?"

When she said this, Derek had blushed for he felt he had offended her. Remembering, he shook his head and placed the cool tooth back under his clothes. "Whatever charm this bit of bone may be," he said, "it will not replace skill and courage when we meet this dragon, Moonstone." He patted the neck of the proud war horse as they rode in the midday sun.

***

Gerald

Gerald smiled as he laid his head against the trunk of the shade tree and rested. He unfolded the scroll the Duchess had given him as his horse Gonrest nibbled grasses at the side of the road. He felt assured that he had lost any followers that might have been spying on him. After all, Derek had a way of being nosy where he was concerned, always suspicious of him just because he didn't understand the way his mind worked. It was certain that Derek could never understand the kind of treasure he sought now. And Max was always poking about where he shouldn't be. Well, Gerald thought, perhaps when he brought back the greatest treasure in the land, they would respect his privacy then. They had better.

He remembered the mystery of the Duchess' words with him when Derek had finally left them that night at the Inn. He had been reading ancient verse to the noblewoman and Derek had excused himself. Gerald grinned. There was nothing better than deep thoughts to send his older brother up to bed. Max of course was already upstairs. As the candlelight of their table burned low, the fireplace of the room settled to glowing embers. They sat alone in the small dining room talking over their drinking goblets. Even the lady's dwarf had fallen asleep in the corner of the room.

"So, I see that while each of you seek a treasure, the treasure *you* desire is not like the ones your brothers pursue."

The Duchess smiled with a glance at the stairs.

Gerald frowned. "What do you say, my lady?"

Her smile was knowing, as if he were joking with her. "Do not *tease* me, young Prince. *We* are not children. Your brothers are kind and good, and noble enough of heart, but treasure means gold and silver to boys of such *simple* vision, shall I say?"

Until that moment Gerald had been thinking only of gold and silver himself. He knew in an instant that she meant something more important, more intelligent. Certainly, it must be the sort of thing he *ought* to be seeking. He had sensed this same spirit of cleverness and intelligence in the lady's words all evening. Now she gave him the first hint of what lay behind her smile. Yes, he alone of the brothers was worthy of such a confidence. His heart leapt with excitement, but he made himself remain calm in appearance. He knew she tested him now and to appear unwise would be to fail.

"Derek and Max are my brothers. It would grieve me that you should think poorly of them," he said. "Of course, they have limited imaginations I am afraid, though it is not their fault. As for myself, I am not certain that I should speak of my own thinking on this matter of treasures, until I know your mind also."

The lady's smile was wide. Gerald knew he had spoken well. "You and I know that true treasure means power. And knowledge. The right kind of knowledge *is* power." She raised her goblet to sip it. "Do you know the kind of knowledge I speak of?"

Gerald swallowed. He did not know how he knew, but he *knew*. It was as if looking into her eyes he was entering a hidden chamber, a forbidden room. He felt no fear, only hunger to be admitted, to be one of those inside — with the knowledge. "Yes," he whispered. "How much power do you speak of?"

Her eyes flashed at his question. He felt for an instant that she might cast him out and deny him the secret he longed for. He shivered. Then she laughed. And it was as if he were forgiven for some small mistake. "Enough," she said. "*More* than enough for all your dreams."

He laughed with her. "Well, that is quite a lot. But how shall I find this treasure, my Lady?"

She tapped her chin. "Have you never heard of the Wise Ones? The old ones under the hills?" She leaned closer again and whispered, "The council of the *Green Fire*?"

Though he had heard many childhood fables, Gerald could remember none of these. Still, he nodded. "Yes. Often, I have wondered if they were true tales, and what could be believed. There are many stories — they are often different."

She placed her gloved hand on his wrist. "Forget all you have ever heard."

Gerald was glad of this, since he had heard nothing, but he would never admit ignorance about anything.

"If you *are* that special one, chosen for a higher purpose, then I serve you with a chance to fit yourself for your calling. With my clues, if you are worthy, you shall find your way into the court of the Wise Ones. If you are indeed wise, you shall be treasured with the power and knowledge that will make you a king of both day *and* night."

When she said this, the sleeping dog under the table stirred and gave a muffled bark as dogs sometimes do when they dream. The dwarf jerked awake at this and Gerald turned to stare at the pop-eyed little man. When he turned back, the Duchess was holding out a small scroll to him.

"It is not wise to speak of such things here," she said. "Take this with you and keep it secret from all others. Follow the way it unfolds and perhaps soon we shall meet again in a *happier* place."

CHAPTER 7

THE FOX TAKES THE LEAD

Leaving the main road Max, Knipper and the sheep followed Fanzig the fox on a narrow trail through the shadows of the forest. As he rode deeper into the woods Max worried at the time he was losing from the quest for his treasure. This new way was even longer than the road he had taken for the shepherd. *Oh, well,* he thought, *this is certainly an adventure — no treasure, but what of talking animals?* He strained to see the way that Fanzig led them. It grew darker and the shadows were turning to night. The trees were crowding in as they followed the twisting bends and Max imagined eyes watched from every bush. He was losing sight of the flock in the twilight when Fanzig padded up.

"This is a safe place to stay tonight," the fox said. "A fire here will not be seen at much distance."

Max was glad to stop. Slipping off Blueberry, he realized they were in a clearing. A silver cloud slipped away from the moon allowing enough light to gather firewood. As they settled to eat around the crackling flames Max listened to the mournful voices of the flock that had moved to a little valley below them to graze. Eating the dry road cake reminded him of the hot suppers he was used to and indeed of much he missed, especially his family. He wondered how his brothers were faring and if they also faced unforeseen dangers. He gazed up at the silent moon and wondered if they perhaps did the same.

Fanzig spoke. "Well, good Max, you know a great deal more about us than most living men. Tell us something of yourself. What brings you to be traveling the roads alone? Forgive me, but you seem a bit young to be an adventurer or knight of the realm."

Max looked across the fire at his two new friends. They were wonderful creatures and great fun to talk with, but still he missed home. He wondered if he should tell them of the adventure. Talking Beasts, after all, might be something a sly witch might use to trick him. He remembered his father's words; *"Trust only those who may be trusted."*

Fanzig spoke again. "Come, come, good Max. Who are you? We are beasts and nothing more, but your life must be full of dangers and fun."

Knipper cocked his head sideways as he often did. "It's sure he's brave and well trained with a sword. I'd like to know how he came to learn that."

Looking into Knipper's kind old face and Fanzig's smiling amber eyes he knew they could not be evil. *"Well,"* he thought, *"if these may not be trusted then none can"*. He set his cup down and wrapped his arms around his knees and told them his story. He told them of his father the king and his two brothers and the search for the greatest treasure in all the land. He told them of the inn and the Duchess and the way she made you listen to her, but he did not tell them of the treasure she had sent him in search of. There was something that did not let him speak of the golden forest and the tree without color. He had gone against *so* many warnings already that he decided to heed just this one. What harm could there be in a single secret, and it did belong to him alone.

When he had finished, Fanzig spoke. "So, you have come a long way from your path to help old Dimbarrel save his flock. You are of noble heart, my lad. Even your brother Derek would not do that."

"Oh, surely he would," Max declared. He was very proud of his oldest brother and did not like to hear him judged wanting.

Fanzig crouched down beside the fire and looked up over the flames. "I have traveled near and far, my young friend, and I know your brother — though he knows me not. He is a good knight, but not more."

Max frowned. "What more could there be than a good knight?"

"One who hears the silent voices as well as the loud. One who knows that evil is not just a dragon or a giant and that glory is not tied to one's lance like a lady's pretty handkerchief. These are things 'we' see but come hard for people. Don't ask why, but that is the way of it." The fox blinked its amber eyes.

Max felt angry, but something in him knew Fanzig spoke a certain truth. Derek knew all sorts of things and had done great deeds. He had taught Max much of sword and horse, but he forgot birthdays and afternoon games and helping with the lessons. He didn't mean to; he just didn't think about it. Max answered, "You would like my brother Gerald, I think. He is clever like you." He didn't really think so, but he was cross at the fox.

Fanzig twitched his thin black snout. "Ah, yes, Gerald. Clever? Yes, I suppose you may call him that, young master. Yet the fox is clever to live, and Gerald lives to be clever." Fanzig saw that Max was confused. "I mean that some things are not good or bad of themselves. Like being happy. I knew a princess once who wished *that* above all else. Everyone wishes that, of course, but she spent all of her time trying only to make herself happy. She played only games she liked, ate only the food she liked, and only talked of things she liked."

"Was she happy?" Max's curiosity drew him out. It was hard to stay angry at Fanzig.

"She was more miserable than anyone I have ever known. You find happiness sharing it with others, Prince Max. When you only care to enjoy yourself, it becomes harder and harder to truly enjoy anything. Being happy alone is like trying to be friends with a mirror. It is not real, but a trick, and a backwards one, too."

Max studied the fox. "You know very much," Max said. "I never heard anyone who spoke more of such things except Father."

"We beasts are given a lot, but we are given it differently and for a different purpose. There are not many of us now." The fox smiled but his eyes were sad.

Knipper rolled out his tongue. "You talk long, Fanzig. At least tell us a story or a poem. A story helps to keep the darkness warm and brings happy rest."

The fox grinned and sat up. "There is one that I have not told in some time." He looked up to the stars and began.

"Do sit back and relax, good friends, I will tell you a legend of the mistletoe. Quiet now — it begins."

"Many and many a year ago, o'er old Gaspaar way,
Bonnie Prince Charles set to hunt upon one Christmas day.
After a weary morning, the prince he fairly cried,
'Come horse, come hound, we'll not slack
till wily fox is spied!'

"Now the world was awash and awattle -
with the hound's bay and the horse's rattle,
and every peasant in the country knew,
'twas Charles' horn alone that blew!

"Deep in the forest, good fox hides -
lives by his wit, Lady at his side.
He takes but silly hens that stray,
and a fat goose only on Christmas day.

"Good fox pricks up his ears to laugh,
'Bonnie Prince Charlie announces his path!'
Lady fox worried turned to say,
'Then to the deep forest, let's away!'

"The chase was long- the chase was hard -
the foxes led them through every yard.
Low branches stung and hounds' tongues droop,
Fox and his Lady led them all a fair loop.

"But then the prince put spurs deep in,

and the hunt set off yet once again!
Fox says, 'Let us to the great oak fly -
we can run the trunk; the leaves may hide!'

"So, the foxes turned and hard they ran,
driven on by the prince's band.
they came to the oak, but now saw -
thick mistletoe wrapped 'round trunk and all,

"grown so thick that none might cling -
not hand nor paw, they could take no wing.
Good fox to vixen turned to cry,
'We're done at last, one kiss, then die.'

"They came on fast, the horse and hound,
and soon the hunt, the tree surround.
The royal prince drew his bow,
sighted the game to fly the blow.

"But to his eye there came a tear.
All the hunt drew quiet to hear.
'Oh, nobles, come with me to kill,
see thou the prey, so brave and still?

"Trapped beyond all hope of miss -
they turn and bid a farewell kiss.
Let no man his arrow fly.
Love so strong should not die!

"The fox is driven here by foe,
but stopped to kiss by mistletoe.
Let such berry on Christmas day -
mark the love we pray will stay!'

*"And so the prince and hunt turned 'round,
and fox and vixen freedom found.
Death would strike love, but must always miss -
and that is remembered with Mistletoe's Kiss."*

"That certainly is a wonderful story," Max said. "Is it true?"

"It is not good manners to ask the storyteller if his story is true," Knipper chided.

Fanzig laughed. "He is right, young Max, but you are forgiven. That story is old, and perhaps it grows longer and better with the telling. But my great grandfather was the first of the talking foxes in Gaspaar, and he told it to me as I told it to you."

"I didn't mean to say I didn't believe it," Max said. "It is just that I have never heard such stories, and I have never had such fun, or such friends. I have never had an adventure before either, but I feel this is a good one and somehow it will all come right at the end, like your story."

Knipper yawned. "It is late, and we should sleep. We can reach the Willtil tomorrow if we rise early."

With that, Max lay down on his blanket, and Knipper settled down facing the flock. They each fell asleep quickly, but Fanzig watched the great yellow moon and thought about the times of his grandfather.

CHAPTER 8

UNDER THE WILLTIL

Max woke with a start the next morning. Something cold and moist brushed against his ear. He opened his eyes to see Knipper gazing at him over a dark snout. The sky was still very dark with only a dim light on the horizon where the sun was going to rise. "Must we get up already?" Max asked.

The dog sat back on its haunches. "The crossing of the Willtil is a long way from here and journey is much easier in the daylight. The sooner we get the sheep home to Dimbarrel's farm, the sooner you can be after your treasure."

Max rubbed the sleep from his eyes. "I guess Derek and Gerald are close to their treasures by now."

"Do you give up so easily?" Knipper chuckled. "An easy adventure is no adventure at all. I'm only a shepherd's dog, but even I know that."

Max frowned but nodded. Sometimes Knipper gave more advice than he wanted. Still, he certainly was learning a lot. The last four days had been different from anything he had experienced in his whole life. He already felt like a different person from the boy who played with his puppy in the stables and slept under fresh clean sheets at night.

They spent the morning traveling through the woods. Max had never seen such a forest. At first it seemed dark and unfriendly, but he began to notice things he had not seen before. Birds called to each other and rabbits watched them from the underbrush. A deer glanced from behind a thicket. A snake hurried to get off its warm rock and out of their way. It occurred to Max that *he* might frighten a snake as much as it might frighten him. He saw that Fanzig was not leading them through a dangerous land of shadows, but through his own familiar kingdom.

In the late afternoon they came out of the forest and with little warning were on the banks of a river. The Willtil was more like a wide creek here with stones jutting up all across its swirling rapids. Beyond the speeding currents on the other side, Max could see the great hills of Gumbor. They rose up like huge green bubbles dotted with rustling spruce trees. They swelled up as far as the eye could see. Only the thick forest branches had kept Max from seeing them before.

The prince wondered how Fanzig intended them to cross the river with no bridge. Even with the many wide stones breaking the surface here the gaps between were too great for a sheep to leap across even if it might be pushed to try. They could never herd an entire flock across this way. He turned to ask the fox but found that Fanzig was still leading them but on a path alongside the bank and then, to Max's surprise, back into the forest. Curious indeed. Entering the forest here he saw that there were many large boulders about, even some taller than a house. As they traveled this way in the opposite direction of the river for several minutes he wondered at his guide's intention.

The fox turned and came back toward the prince. "We are here," he said.

Max leaned forward on his saddle. "I see nothing but trees and boulders."

The fox nodded. "And so, it should remain to most eyes. Do you see the shadow beneath the tallest stone, the one shaped like a large pear?"

"Yes," Max replied. "But what of it?"

"Follow me," his guide said and headed toward the rock.

Max followed but pulled Blueberry to a sudden halt when Fanzig disappeared before his very eyes. One moment the fox was there in the shade of the boulder and the next instant he had vanished completely. Max got down off the pony and stepped carefully into the shadow. He stretched his arms out in front of him. Just as he expected to touch stone, he felt only a cool breeze in the darkness. He had walked past the wall of the rock. This was the mouth of a cave.

"Yes," Fanzig's voice echoed from nearby, "a tunnel beneath the river, good Max. It was hollowed out many years ago when the river ran somewhere else. This secret tunnel angles up into the hills on the far side. One day the river changed course and it became an underground bridge. It won't last much longer. The water will cut through the ceiling someday soon. For now, it is a secret of the forest and the elves."

"The elves?" Max asked in an excited whisper. He had wondered if there really were such beings. He had heard many stories as a child, but no one he knew had actually seen one. Now anything seemed possible.

"Yes, there are elves. They don't travel much among the Tall Ones, as they call your people. They know the woods as even the beasts themselves. They have journeyed here before. There are elf markings in the tunnel."

"We will need some light." Knipper's voice joined them. "I don't believe the lambs will go in without any light."

"I'll make some torches," Max said. "Derek taught me how." He looked back at the cave as he stumbled into the daylight again. "I'm afraid I wouldn't want to go in without a light either."

It took a little while to get everything set. Max found tree sap clumped in yellow blobs on a few pines nearby. It was harder to cut up the green branches to hold pinecones to serve as wicks. Smearing the cones with the sticky resin went well enough but he wondered how many he might need as he knew they would take at least two or three in an hour of dark travel. He asked Fanzig of the tunnel's length.

"Well, I have traveled it once and it is quite long on the uphill side, I believe there are cracks above that may let in a bit of light and rain."

Max nodded. "Well, it's taken me nearly as long to make the torches as we can hope for them to burn. Let's hope your fox eyes can lead us if it is not long enough!"

The sheep didn't like where Knipper was herding them. Even Fanzig had to help round up strays that darted away at the last instant. The fox came up out of breath with a frightened lamb scampering before him. "Whew!" he panted, "I only run this hard to catch dinner."

"It's a good thing the sheep don't understand your words," Knipper said. "You would have to chase that one all over again."

They laughed at that, but Max felt a little nervous as they lined up. Presently, Fanzig turned to him.

"Well, Max, I am afraid this tunnel is as much of this land as I know. I can tell you little of the hills beyond. I know the way is dangerous and there are tales of giants. But when you set out upon an adventure, you set yourself against all odds. I am at your service as long as you wish it, but I do not pretend to truly know what lies ahead."

Max swallowed. "At least we have escaped a band of robbers who would have taken the sheep and murdered us. That is one danger we have gotten by."

The fox grinned. "There is an old saying; *'For every day there is a way.'* I believe you will find it, Max, if you will look for it and not give up hope."

Knipper barked. "Enough of this. We know the hills of Gumbor are strange. Any land is strange to those who have never traveled it. If we are to turn back now, then let's do it. If we are to go on, then let's go on." Despite the brave words, Max knew that Knipper was worried.

"All right then," Max said. "Let's start. But stay within sight of each other." He had lit a torch with the flint from his tender box and now carried it as he walked into the shadow. A nervous Blueberry paced behind him. She nuzzled his back and kept close to him. "*Anything might be in here,*" Max thought, "*snakes, lizards, even bats.*" He shivered a little when he thought of that, but he was already well in and the others were following.

Inside the cave the air was cool and moist. As his eyes

grew used to the light of the torch, Max could see that water dripped from the ceiling here and there as they angled downward to cross beneath the river. None of them said a word and even the sheep seemed to keep quiet as they moved along. A rolling sound began to grow about them. Max stopped.

"The Willtil is just above us," Fanzig said.

Blueberry's sudden snort boomed down the cold dark walls.

"How far does the cave go?" Max whispered.

"A good way yet. And the longest bit is uphill," the fox replied, also in a whisper.

They started moving again until Blueberry clapped her hooves in a frightened shuffle on the rocky floor. The sharp echoes clattered around them.

"What is it, girl?" Max stared into the dark ahead.

"*What is it, indeed?*" A strange voice answered him from the darkness beyond. Before Max could even grab his sword, a thin little man clad in forest green stepped into the torch light. "What indeed are you doing on the elves' road?"

Max knew without doubt that the little man could only be an elf. His face was round and trimmed with a sharp black beard that curled upwards into twin points. His eyes were a grey-green color that sparkled in the flickering light and his ears rose into distinct points, like little wings against his head. A tight leather cap covered his hair and cut back sharply to leave room for his ears. He was a small man — even smaller than Max—but he seemed fierce and dangerous. Max was so amazed that he forgot to say anything. Brandishing a short, jeweled knife, the elf thundered out his stern challenge again.

"Speak, lad. Have you no tongue or wits? This is not the road of common shepherds. What business have a flock of sheep and a witless boy on the elves' roadway? Answer me quick or I'll clip off your ears." When he said this, he twirled the little dagger in his hand and Max saw the emeralds and rubies of the hilt glitter in the torchlight.

Fanzig's voice came from behind Max. "Stay your blade, good elf. Our young shepherd comes as a friend of the forest folk. Besides, I know of his sword-play and it could well be *your* fine ears which were snipped." The fox had come up beside Max now and Knipper was with him.

Max felt better with his companions nearby and Fanzig's voice had put him at ease. He answered the elf. "Please, sir, I only came this way because robbers wait for us at the river bridge. I have no thought of betraying its secret."

The elf wrinkled his heavy brows. "It's not usual to see the speaking beasts so free with a Tall One. I suppose there is a tale here and I mean to hear it. Yet, since you are already on the road, I suppose you may follow it. But you'd best tell no man of this way if you value your life." When he finished, the elf turned around without waiting for a reply. His green cloak, with a thin carved bow strapped across one shoulder, vanished ahead in the darkness almost at once.

Max gazed after him. "I wonder how he can move along so quickly without a torch?"

Knipper scratched his ear with a hind paw. "Oh, elves can see in the dark as well as an owl or bat. He sees his way better in here than we do, that much is certain."

They started again and as they continued it fast became a climb as Fanzig had said. The floor began to slant up almost like one of the great hills above them. After some time, they could smell fresh air coming from somewhere. Max knew his torches would soon be finished. He hoped he should not be without them. "Surely we must soon see daylight," he said.

"I doubt you will find it outside, just now," Knipper

replied. "The sun was near setting when we entered, you know. Probably evening out there by now. We've gone far beyond the river."

Soon the dog was proven right. As Max saw the final flame of his torch flickering low, he brushed against something that rustled and shook. It startled him for just an instant. "It's a tree. We're outside," he gasped.

It was true. Looking around him Max could see that they were in the middle of a small stand of spruce trees. The moon waited above them.

For the second time the elf's voice came from the darkness. "I would stamp out that torch if I were you." He was sitting beneath a tree with his legs crossed under him and his hands on his knees.

"Why?" asked Max when he saw the speaker.

"There may be few robbers in the hills of Gumbor but more likely a giant or two. You are on one of the taller hilltops and even that flicker might be seen for miles by such large eyes."

Max smothered the torch with handfuls of dirt and tramped out the tiny sparks. He didn't like the idea of meeting a giant in the dark. Once he had extinguished the embers, he could tell that the moonlight was bright enough to see well by. He turned to Knipper. "Do you think you could find a good place for the sheep?"

"This hillside is as good as any in Gumbor," the elf volunteered.

The dog sniffed the air and nodded. "I'll lead them out of the trees away from the hilltop."

As Knipper moved the flock smoothly down the hill, pushing a hesitant lamb here and nosing another there, the elf spoke again. "Now, you will tell me your reasons for traveling the elf road."

Max sat down and leaned back against a narrow tree trunk. He didn't realize how tired he was until he sat down. "Well," he began, "I am Max, and I am on something of an adventure. My path has been blocked by robbers who tried to steal my friend's sheep. My plan is to take them to his farm in the Runruggel Mountains. Fanzig here is the one who has led me on this road."

The elf's eyes twinkled in the moonlight. "I suppose that since the speaking beasts are friends to you, I also should trust you. That is something I have learned not to do often. Trusting is the end of the elf. We have survived so long because we have kept our secrets secret. I can see that you have not told me everything. That is good. Long stories are not easily believed."

Max wondered at the bitterness of the elf's words. "Please, sir, you know my name and something of my journey. Could you tell us a little of yourself?"

Fanzig added, "It is only fair."

The elf squinted and nodded. "So be it. My name is Jippit Jumpjilter and I am leaving the land of you Tall Ones forever. I am traveling the long and secret road to Elfenland to join the court of my fathers. If you think for an instant that I am going to tell you where that is, you are very mistaken. We elves would gladly lay down our lives before we would tell anyone of the secret way to our homeland."

Max shook his head. "No. I am not asking that. It is enough for me that there *is* a land of elves. But tell me, why are you leaving with such anger?"

The little man popped the knuckles of his long thin fingers. "You have me talking quite a bit, young Max. That is something I had not planned on doing this side of the far sea. But I will tell you. I was for a time the court jester of King Lull in the land of Leorna."

"Leorna," Max said. "It lies north of the Lumbadil and east of the Shaleen doesn't it?"

"You know a little geography then. That is good if you mean to travel the lands. Yes, I was the jester for old King Lull and his gang — may they rot."

Max could not imagine this sulking elf as a court jester, clowning and joking for a hall of nobles. "Why are you so against them? Didn't you make them laugh?"

"Laugh? Yes, they laughed all right, but not at my jokes. They laughed at *me*! They thought *I* was quite funny. Odd things tickled their fancy, like a two-headed cow or a five-legged dog." The elf struck his hand in a fist, "They laughed at me because I was an *elf*. An elf of royal blood!"

When Jippit finished, Max was quiet for a moment. He felt awkward. "I am sorry," he said, "King Lull can't be very wise if he laughs at you. Father says that differences have a purpose. He says the more differences you understand, the wiser you are. That if everyone were alike, they wouldn't be very happy. I'm sorry King Lull doesn't understand."

The elf's heavy eyebrows scrunched together. "Who are you, young Max? Who is your father and what is your journey? I know you are no common lad and certainly no simple shepherd's boy. By the clouds of Izmah, who are you?"

Max cleared his throat. "I am the son of King Randrew of Gaspaar. I seek the greatest treasure in all the land." Max swallowed hard when he said this. He was trusting the little man more than perhaps he should. Now the elf would want to know where the treasure was. *Don't worry, Duchess,* he said to himself, *I have said enough. When my road turns back to the East, I will travel it alone.*

The elf had been silent when Max answered his questions. Now he spoke almost in a whisper. "The Prince of Gaspaar. I would have guessed it."

That's hardly true, Max thought to himself, but said, "Only one of the princes. I have two brothers and they are seeking such treasure as well."

"Ahhh, what treasure might it be that needs a flock of sheep to find it?" the elf smiled a sly smile.

Max almost told him but caught himself. "You *would* like to know that, would you? I take the road I please, and few suspect a shepherd as a prince."

Jippit Jumpjilter nodded, still grinning. "Well said. I have no desires for treasure myself. In Elfenland treasures are used for doorstops and boat anchors. I just wondered that you would risk your life against giants and robbers for mere gold and silver. This treasure must be something quite wonderful. But now you seem to be running an errand instead of trying to find it. Odd. Very odd, indeed."

The elf's comments worried Max more than a little. He wondered if he could really trust this Jumpjilter. He had always imagined that elves would be honest folk, yet he was learning to be more careful. Things were not always as they seemed.

And so, passed Max's first night in the legendary hills of Gumbor. He did not sleep well. He was certain he heard giants all night long. Just when he would be nearly asleep, a lamb would cry out, or an owl would hoot in the distance. He knew these hills were not friendly and that he would be more than happy when morning came.

CHAPTER 9

PATHS OF FATE

Breakfast was better than Max might have hoped. Jippit had gone off early and caught some fish in a nearby stream. The sizzling and popping over the elf's fire woke the prince. He rubbed the sleep from his eyes and sniffed the aroma of frying fish. His stomach rumbled.

"The Royal Belly awakes," the elf said. "Will your Highness be rising for breakfast?"

Max looked around, ignoring the elf's joke. "Where are Knipper and Fanzig?"

"They've gone to fetch the sheep. Something frightened them last night, so Knipper moved them over the far rise there. You must have been very sound asleep. I was sure no one could rest through their racket." The elf turned the fish on the stick above the fire.

"You should have waked me." Max was embarrassed at not having been more alert.

"Ho! Ho! I suppose you would have run off any giants that came upon us," the elf grinned. "The dog tells me you are quite a swordsman."

Max looked away to the rise as Knipper herded the sheep towards them. "I guess I've learned a few things," he said. "I know not to pick a fight."

When they had finished breakfast, Max tied his bed roll on Blueberry's saddle and climbed up. Everyone seemed uneasy. Max could tell that Knipper was nervous by the way he kept after the lambs, not letting them wander the least bit. Everyone was thinking of the giants. Max looked out over the tall round hills. *How easily they might hide a crouching monster.* He was almost sure he had seen something move out of the corner of his eye. Yet turning to look, there was nothing.

The prince felt foolish. Here he was, miles from the treasure he sought, and going farther from it with every step into a strange and dangerous land. All this for an old man he hardly knew. He could never explain it to Gerald.

Max looked down at the sheep. They were restless too, peering in all directions as if aware of some waiting danger. They were not anything like the speaking beasts, but Max had grown fond of them. He enjoyed the playfulness of the lambs and admired the dignity of the older sheep. Well, they were in his hands now and he realized that their safety meant more than just the favor to old Dimbarrel. *Probably no more than a single bite to a giant,* Max shuddered.

"Well, Master Max," Jippit Jumpjilter said, "are you

having doubts about journeying through the land of the giants? The tunnel that you followed here leads back to the forest as well, you know."

Perhaps Jippit saw his thoughts only too well. Max sat straight in his saddle and frowned at the taunting figure. "I am quite ready to begin, thank you. Do you wish to travel with us? I see you have on your pack. I suppose traveling together is a bit safer than going on *alone* to Elfenland?"

The little man glowered. "*Safe*? Ha! I was alone before you came and alone, I shall go, but our roads run together here. Besides, someone should watch out for you. I would feel quite ashamed if a giant gobbled you up only because I had not the decency to guide you. Never reject the aide of your betters, young Max. We elves seldom befriend Tall Ones anymore."

Before Max could answer this Knipper turned around. "Isn't it time we were going? This is not a road I have traveled, and I don't like it. Let's make no more enemies in Gumbor than we might already have."

Max felt his face flush at the dog's words. "Knipper is right, Master Jumpjilter. I do not wish to insult you. I am glad to have your aid in this place. Even Fanzig says he knows little of the way here. Lead us on, if you will. We are in your debt."

The elf did not answer but slung his cape over his shoulder, arranged his bow over his back, and grasped his staff before marching to the head of the little company. He turned around and snapped, "Follow me at an arrow shot's distance. I shall need to be a little ahead, but mind you make no noises. Giants have very large ears." With that he turned again, and they set off.

***

Derek

Nearing the town of Low Arden at the border of Averon, Prince Derek rested Moonstone on a hill overlooking the busy crossroads. He patted the gold charger and felt beneath his shirt for the tooth the Duchess had given him.

"Still cold, Moonstone. If Gerald knew I chased dragons with a tooth for luck, he would call me a fool or worse. Stories told by candlelight seem less solid in sunlight. These days of riding had best prove the lady's tale more than a pretty jest. I have staked much on this quest with nothing to show but this nasty trinket. By heaven, it looks the tooth of an old grandfather plucked out for rot. Still, I suppose a dragon's *baby* tooth might age with such heat as its fire must make. Here's a pretty thing, Low Arden's wall is topped with a dragon weathervane. I'll have the story of that, you may be sure, as well as a good bed and stable tonight."

The guard at the gate recommended a lodging for the lone knight. He nodded when Derek pointed to the weathervane and asked how it came to be. "Bless me, sire, it's told that this wall was the line drawn against the dragons in the days of old. Averon's kings fought them back, if you believe the granny tales. They say the lands up north towards the sea still pay tribute to dragons and worse. But that's Empt for you; a sad and solitary kingdom where good things go bad and sickness floats on the wind. Blaming dragons seems a poor excuse. It may be that those stories are all told for the defense of the land. Who would want to conquer a country with a dragon hidden in its reaches? Why it'd be like buying a house filled with rats."

Derek frowned. "You may speak truly friend, but I am on a quest. If such a creature still infests Empt and the village of Kurn, then I am bound by honor to rid them of their *rat*."

Gerald

Prince Gerald noted that a stone well had now appeared on his scroll as he rode. This was truly an enchanted map, for the way was drawn with signs and instruction found as one traveled. However, the signs and words were only visible as he moved forward. He saw that the path once followed faded away when passed. Only as he neared the next point did the way beyond it begin to grow visible on the map. Each day the way was open, but only for that day. The Duchess had warned that once followed, the map was useless; that to move away from its path would erase its every line and clue.

The prince looked again as the details filled in. Stacked stones formed, as if by an invisible pen, into the rounded sides of the well. Wooden beams were drawn supporting a winding bar and handle. Last to fill out were the thick rope and the sturdy bucket that it held. Words scrolled out beside the drawing which Gerald read aloud:

"Do as you are bid, and drink deeply of what lies beneath."

The prince frowned. "Do as I am *bid*? Drink from this well?" Riding over the rise of the hill, he saw in the next valley that a stone well did wait beside the path. There were no trees or shrubs near this structure. It did not occur to Gerald that such a source of water should evidence life around it. The path was dusty, and Gerald felt his thirst grow as he neared the bucket which swung in a light breeze. "Truly I could use a full drink now," he sighed. Nearing the well Gonrest snorted and came to a sudden halt. "What is it?" Gerald would have struck his riding crop against the horse's flank but saw a gray cat slink out from the back of the well-stones and sit on its haunches as if to greet him.

"Fie, fine horse," Gerald grunted. "You frighten at a tabby? Well, I'll have *my* drink first." He had intended to bring up a bucket for his horse, as the brothers had learned to care for their horses from their earliest days. Stepping down from his saddle, the prince walked to the edge of the well to grip the bucket. He felt the cat attempt a lazy back rub against his leg and scooted it to the side with his boot. Looking down into the well, he was surprised to see that it was deeper than he had imagined. Too deep and dark to see the bottom. "This had best be a long rope," he complained.

Behind him Gonrest gave a sudden whinny. He turned to see what had spooked the horse, which was retreating up the path. He shouted after it, but a smooth voice behind him seized his attention.

"I shouldn't worry about your horse, young master. He'll amble back when he's thirsty enough."

Gerald spun round to find an old man in a gray robe with a long, dusty beard, blinking at him over crossed arms. The elder's eyes were shaded under a wide brimmed and pointy hat. For an instant, between blinks, Derek thought his pupils were thin slits like those of a cat. But when his eyes opened again, they were merely plain and brown, and a little yellow under his worn, wrinkled brows.

"And who are you, might I ask?" Gerald was disturbed at the sudden appearance of the man, who seemed to have sprung from out of nowhere.

"Forgive me, young sire. I am just one who thirsts, as you, for that which lies below this well. I was resting here against the stones. I am sorry if I have frightened you."

Gerald frowned. "I am not frightened, old sir, merely curious at how you come to be here, and how it is you have not quenched your thirst. Do you wait for it to grow greater?"

The old man chuckled. "Ah, but this is a *deep* well. It takes two to bring up the drink that waits below. One to lower, and one to ride the bucket down and move to the fountain inside the hill."

Gerald stared. "And you wish me to lower you down?"

"Nay, sire. I may handle the crank well enough. With your strong back you may bring us up a brimming bucket. You will have to seek the fountain down a twisting way when you have reached the bottom. There is a path of stones, for you to follow."

Gerald laughed. "You'd have me trust a stranger to lower me into the Earth? Into the deepest well I've ever seen, and pursue a fountain in a cavern below? Why, if fool enough to agree, I would stumble in the dark, for I've no torch for such adventure." He remembered a weird tale of a tinder box and strange underground chambers. "Next you shall tell me that there are treasure rooms and dogs with eyes the size of plates." Yet even as he bantered with the old man, he knew he would go down, and his very arguments were like warning signs he had already passed.

"Sire need not worry," the old man smiled. "There is a light there below. A green glowing light will lead you. I bid you ride down and drink deep of what awaits."

CHAPTER 10

IN THE HILLS OF GUMBOR

The morning was brisk and dark clouds hid the sun. Gumbor's hills were deep, hard green in the gray light. It was so quiet that the travelers heard the wind rushing across the grass on the far sides of them. The only other sound; the bleating of the sheep. The little band worked their way from valley to valley, avoiding hilltops whenever they could. On hilltops they could be seen for miles.

Max noticed that he heard no birds. On this side of the Willtil there were no songbirds and no songs. Time dragged on their silent journey and Max wondered how long it would take to cross the hills of Gumbor. He did not wish to spend another night there. At least Jumpjilter seemed to know exactly where he was going. The elf never slowed or said a word as he led them on. Max was curious at this strange fellow and since thinking about Jippit took his mind off giants, he thought about him very hard.

Later when the clouds above were brightest and Max supposed it near noon, the wind died. The sheep got quiet and a strange feeling settled on them all. He saw that Blueberry's ears were up straight and that Knipper had raised his snout to sniff the air. "I don't like it," Max whispered to himself.

"Neither do I." It was Fanzig trotting along beside him. The fox moved with such stealth that he surprised the prince when he spoke.

"What do you suppose it is?" Max asked as he searched the hilltops.

"I'm afraid it is not good. Perhaps we are frightened of nothing, but I have had this feeling before, when the hunter bends his bow."

Max shivered. "It makes me wish we were in the tunnel again."

The fox nodded. "I have scouted about and can see nothing. My eyes have never beheld a giant, but I believe I would recognize one if I saw it."

Max chuckled without joy. "And I hope you never do. I guess the elf would be the first to know if we were being followed by an enemy. And he hasn't said a thing or even slowed down."

"He may not want to worry us," Fanzig replied. "I am afraid he does not think we are very brave warriors."

"*If only we were,*" Max thought.

Knipper joined them. "The sheep are too quiet. This is

not good. I think we might do well to look for some shelter.”

“I shall speak to Jumpjilter.” Max agreed and trotted Blueberry ahead near to the elf's side. Jippit did not look up as the prince matched his pace. “Excuse me, Master Jumpjilter,” he said, “but do *you* feel we are in danger?”

The elf did not turn his eyes from the way before him as he answered. “A giant has been 'earing' us for nearly an hour if that is what you mean.”

“What?” Max was surprised as much by the elf's seemingly careless attitude as at his frightening words. “You mean a giant has been hearing us and you have not warned us?”

“*Earing* us,” Jumpjilter corrected. “Listening to our footsteps from miles away. He presses his ear to the earth and the hills speak to him like great hollow drums.” The elf looked up as he continued but did not stop walking. “Besides, what would you have done? The giant is listening, he is not coming — yet.”

“Surely we could seek some shelter!”

The guide sounded almost bored as he replied. “There is none here. The giant will not come until he is sure of where we are and where we are going. It takes some time for him to read the sounds of the hills. That is why we are still alone now.”

“Then why don't we stop and wait?” Max demanded. “If our feet make no sounds, perhaps he would give up.”

“You do not know giants, young Max,” Jippit said. “When the noise stops, *then* he will soon come. He thinks his prey is tired or asleep and easier to catch. He is waiting for us to stop now.”

Max was becoming very scared but did not want to show it. “What if we don't stop until we are out of Gumbor?”

The elf's laugh was bitter. “*That* is a great distance.

Even if we did, the giant would know what we were doing when night fell, and we did not stop. Then he would come, and we would be too tired to run."

"Then it is not *possible* to escape?"

Jippit walked on for some time before he answered. "There *should* be *another* tunnel in Gumbor. Another tunnel of the elf-road."

"Is it near?" Max was afraid to hope.

Jippit frowned stern-faced. "Let us hope so."

"Then you don't *know*?" Max felt his anger rising.

"I have never traveled this road myself," Jippit replied.

Max did not know whether he was more angry or more frightened. "I thought you were going *home* to Elfenland. You mean you have never even been there? How do you know the way at all?"

Jumpjilter scowled up at Max as he walked. "Elfenland is home to all elves, though not *all* are born there. The road is made known to every elf, from father to son to grandson."

"You tricked us! You acted as if you knew your way! Who was the last of your family to travel this secret road?"

Jippit nearly stopped walking to answer. "I did not *trick* you. I told you some things and not others. That is the way of elves. You have guessed too much from it on your own. My grandfather was the last Jumpjilter to travel this way if you must know. But don't worry about that, *elves* do not change their stories as they are retold. The way has opened to us so far."

Max knew it did no good to lose his temper or to blame the small man for the danger that he had accepted of his own will by stepping into these hills. He did not want to apologize but there was no room for wrongheadedness here. He bit his lip before he spoke again. "I'm sorry I have blamed you for things you could not help," he said. "You are our guide, master elf . . . and if we meet danger . . . we are at your side as well."

Jippit said nothing in reply but nodded and resumed his pace.

Max slowed Blueberry and waited for Fanzig and Knipper. He told them of all that was said. The prince saw that they did not appear terribly upset nor as frightened as he had expected they should be.

"At least we are in noble adventure," Fanzig cocked his head with a wry look. "A hunter's arrow is not so exciting as a wild giant of Gumbor. Just think, we may all become legend someday."

"Who would tell it?" Knipper replied in his tired, matter-of-fact way of speaking. "I don't think giants make legends of their dinners."

Fanzig laughed. "I mean if we escape, of course!"

Max forced himself to smile, envious of the beasts' courage. "I pray we will," he said, though his voice sounded a little more strained than he had meant it to.

"Always a wise plan," the fox smiled. "Who knows? There are four of us and only one giant, I hope. He is outnumbered at least."

"There are four of us, and forty sheep," Knipper said, "and they are getting tired. They will need to rest soon."

Max eyed the straggling flock that looked to be slowing as the afternoon wore on. Jippit Jumpjilter had not slackened his pace and was far ahead. "If the giant comes, I should not blame the elf if he ran on to save himself," he said.

Fanzig and Knipper looked to each other. The fox spoke. "Young Prince, that is a true elf ahead of us. Though he is much angry and unsettled in himself, he has an elf's heart in him. He may plot and plan, but the courage of the elves is legendary. It is not good to doubt a friend so easily."

Max was surprised. "A friend? You have heard all his rough words. Why do you call him a friend? Getting to Elfenland is all *he* cares for, and he does not want our company *there*."

Knipper shook a fly from his floppy ears. "He had no reason to lead us, but he does. He had no reason to travel slowly with us through such dangerous ground, but he does. I call that a friend."

"He seems so bitter and cross with everyone," Max said. "I have never met such a contrary fellow."

Fanzig answered him. "Again, you listen only to his words, as he would have you. Contrary he may be, but he risks much for our safety. To know this elf, you must listen to his *deeds*."

In the long hours that followed, they spoke little as they followed Jippit Jumpjilter into the growing twilight. The sheep made tired noises as they plodded on in the rising dark. Max was falling asleep on Blueberry's back and Knipper had to keep going after lambs that went to sleep on the path. This was the worst night yet. They must not stop though it was certain the giant should soon know they were running away. Then it would come. Still, it would be harder for the giant to find them in the dark, while Jippit, having the eyes of an elf, was able to lead them very well.

They were hardly moving when the clouds began to grow light again. Gazing blurry-eyed over Blueberry's mane, Max saw that Jippit had stopped. He wondered if the elf had finally and truly lost the way. Whatever the case, he knew they must rest soon no matter what distance remained. He began to think of desperate plans to fight the giant.

Jippit stood waiting for them to reach him. "We rest now." he said.

Max wanted to sleep more than anything, but asked,

"Won't the giant come?"

"He comes already. Now we must rest so we may run when he is here."

Max and the Beasts looked at each other.

Jippit continued. "Perhaps he will be too tired from his running to catch us all if we are well rested. Perhaps the tunnel is near enough, perhaps . . . but that is not an elf word."

Max knew Jippit could run much faster without them. "You might reach the tunnel, at least," he said, "if you left us now."

The elf did not blink. "I need my rest also. There is still some time for planning."

With that they all went to a cluster of trees and lay down. The sheep settled at once and needed no watching.

Knipper yawned. "Shouldn't one of us stay awake in case it comes soon?"

"The giant will wake us without any help," Jippit said and turned over to sleep.

Max could never remember being so tired, too tired to even feel afraid. Maybe that is why he settled on his plan. He thought for a long time and decided finally that it was the only way. Getting up, he called to Blueberry. The horse lay on her side, but on hearing Max, rose and shuffled to the prince.

"I am sorry, girl," Max whispered, stroking her muzzle. "I know you are tired, but we must run very hard if we are to save the others." He began to saddle his drowsy mount.

Fanzig was awake and watched as Max laid the saddle blanket on Blueberry's back. "What is your plan, young master?"

Max was afraid to stop for even a moment. He answered as he tied Blueberry's girth. "The giant will be here soon and is sure to catch us. He listens for any sound we make. If he should hear a loud hammering of hooves speeding away, he would think we were escaping. I think he would follow. I shall ride as quickly as I can from here to the north. When you are sure he is chasing us, then you must lead the flock away as fast as you can." The saddle was ready.

The fox's eyes shone with fondness and sadness. "It is a good plan, Max. It may work. But you may be caught alone, or perhaps lost in these strange hills."

Max saw that his hands were shaking as he spoke. "I have been thinking. It is the only way the sheep may escape. This is not the elf's business, but I believe he will see the flock home if I do not return. You and Knipper were right about him."

"You are brave, young Max, and that I knew already. Now I see you are becoming wise as well. These things together are right and rare."

Jippit Jumpjilter rolled over. "Our rest will be shorter than I had hoped. Already the ground tells me a giant is coming quickly." He saw that Max was standing ready to mount Blueberry. "What are you doing?" he asked. "If you run, the giant will hear you escape."

Max told his plan.

Jippit agreed. "It might work. It may well be our only chance. There is only one thing wrong. It should be I who go. I know the ways of giants better."

Max smiled. "How many have you met?"

The elf turned red. "Well — none really, but their ways are passed from father to son to grandson. I know their ways."

"I don't doubt you, Master Jumpjilter. But you must lead the flock if I don't return. I don't know these hills."

Jippit pulled at his beard. "I am no shepherd."

Max climbed onto the saddle. "Will you lead them for me if I am lost? I have no right to ask it of you, but I do as a friend. Answer fast, for even I can hear the giant now."

Sure enough, they all heard the heavy pounding in the

distance as mighty feet rushed on. The flock made frightened cries and Knipper had to bite a few to keep them from running off. Now they felt the ground rumble beneath them and each of the travelers looked at the others but said nothing. No words could tell their feelings at this terror.

Max thought of being home playing in the stables dreaming of such adventures. How different were dreams when they came true.

When they could hear nothing but the slamming of the giant's steps and the ground shook so hard the sheep tumbled to the ground, Jippit grasped Max's arm and bellowed to be heard.

"Run hard! Avoid the hilltops! Lie close to the earth when you hide!"

Max looked back over his shoulder but could still see nothing. He waved once to his friends and put his heels to Blueberry's sides. The already frightened yearling bolted away.

Now the world seemed nothing but the booming footfalls of the approaching giant and the silences between each step. Then Max heard singing. The giant's voice was loud and crude and what he sang drove into Max's heart like a cold spike.

"You may shout, and you may clout,
but you never will get out.
You'll soon be meat on Willie's table!

You can sing and you can dance,
but you still won't have a chance.
You'll soon be meat on Willie's table!

Knights and Knaves all have stumbled,

Max leaned forward and rocked his arms with the horse's strides. He had raced alone at home on open pastures, but these hills were steep and pitched him about. Soon he was hugging Blueberry's neck just to keep from falling off as they galloped. He did not need to coax the frightened pony to speed. Blueberry was running faster than she ever had. They knew no direction, only away from the thundering giant. Glancing over his shoulder, Max caught sight of the giant for the first time. He could see only the monster's head, which looked like an evil, carved pumpkin's face, on the horizon. Then the shoulders and arms of the towering hunter rose over the hills behind them. The giant's head was as large as a small house and he stood taller than the castle walls. His hands were like hay carts. The prince knew this creature might swallow a man whole. He was so frightened he forgot about his plan for the giant to follow them — and that it was working very well. The giant seemed to be listening rather than watching as it followed. It turned its head first one way and then another. Its ears were as large as stable doors.

They ran on for mile after mile; Max knowing the giant must catch them. Yet it hesitated each time it drew near. Just when he began to hope, the monster stamped the earth with a mighty foot. The ground seemed to roll as Max and Blueberry tumbled end over end. The horse was so tired she could not get up. The prince lay panting on his back knowing he would die at any moment.

High above them the giant roared a question. "What have you done with the sheep?" The huge unshaven face scowled down at them. "You have tricked me! Willie comes for mutton! Tasty muttons! I followed the sheep and they ran! But you are here! Where are the sheep?!" He bent low and his sour breath and jagged teeth froze the words in Max's throat.

Max closed his eyes and hoped he would feel no long pain when death came.

"I will crush you for your trick!" the giant roared. He raised his huge foot again, but then stopped and turned his shaggy head. His flat gray eyes narrowed, and a cruel smile spread across his flaking lips. "Ahhh! Willie hears them. Willie hears all the dear little muttons! Here I come, my lamb chops!"

Max watched in fascinated horror as the massive figure got down on its hands and knees. Willie pressed a huge floppy ear to the earth. He could tell the giant was '*earing*' the flock as Jippit had told him. For the first time Max thought he just might live, after all. He slid to Blueberry's shivering side and whispered encouragement in her ear. They rose together and stood in silence, watching. The giant was paying them no attention. His thoughts were only of the "muttons" as he called the flock. Step after careful step, Max led Blueberry into a small valley. At the bottom was a narrow stream and a clump of trees. As they crept down the hillside, he could hear the giant's heavy breathing.

"Aaaahhh, Mutton! Willie wants mutton! What? What's that? elf's feet? Willie hasn't had elf meat for many winters! Tasty! Tasty! Delicious elf and mutton! Much better than stringy horse and a bite of boy!"

Max shuddered at that remark but kept leading Blueberry into the trees. "Shelter," he whispered to himself. "*If* Willie doesn't bother to search hard."

Then, without warning, the giant uttered a great shout and Max and Blueberry stood as still as statues beneath the low hanging branches. The giant was standing again. Willie's head and shoulders were visible above the hill they had walked down.

"Boys and horses!" roared the giant, "who needs them, when sheep and elves are waiting?" With that he turned and fast disappeared. Booming footsteps shook the earth as he rushed back after the flock.

Max sat down with his back against a tree. "Well, Blueberry," he said, "I don't know what more we can do. Perhaps they will find the tunnel before Willie finds them. Maybe we can find it too. How hungry I am — but no, I am even more tired." He lay down and went to sleep; his first sleep in two days of marching.

CHAPTER 11

WHAT MUST BE DONE

Gerald found it difficult to measure passing time since he had entered the underground chambers to taste of the hidden fountain. Only candles lit this new world. Sleep was an uncertain state, for waking here felt much the same. He remembered the green fountain — how long ago was that? — which he had seen when he had reached the bottom of the well; he had bent to cup the cool liquid to his lips. There was a metal taste, a hint of mint also, a thickness that was not disagreeable, yet not so fine as he had imagined it to be. After the first drink he dipped his face into the fountain's pool. Rising to take a deep breath he was surprised to find that the light grew brighter about him and saw that the Duchess stood across from him, smiling, waiting.

"My Lady! Is this indeed you or is this some illusion like the markers on your magic map? Are you real or spirit?"

The Duchess laughed. "We meet again, dear Prince. You have followed well the guide given you. I trust your thirst is quenched?"

Gerald wiped his mouth. "My thirst for drink is quenched. My thirst for those things of which we spoke at the inn is greater than ever. Will you now share that knowledge with me?"

"Patience, dear Gerald. Patience is the first rule of pupils. I have brought you to your teacher; one who has labored years to transcend the bounds of this world. You must prove yourself by following his instruction. I shall visit you often. I eagerly await the time that you are able to join me on the deeper path."

Gerald frowned. "I thought that I should attend *you* and learn firsthand those things whose shape I sensed when we spoke at the inn."

The Lady's eyelids drew lower as she answered. "That is when I also sensed the connection of our minds. Yet, such a thing can only come when its time is ripe. I have much to attend, dear Prince, and we must now be parted. The time we shall next meet will depend upon your progress. I hope you shall not fail me?"

Her brows shaped a look of worried doubt which tormented Gerald's mind. He must not disappoint her.

***

Max

Waking, Max had no idea how long he had slept. The sky was darker, but it might have been days since the wild chase across the hills. He hurt with hunger and knew he must eat something before anything else. Pulling a cheese from his pack he sliced off a large piece. It could not last much longer and he decided to eat it before it spoiled. There were some strips of dried beef and he chewed hard on these also. Even though the meal was cold and stale, it cut his hunger and his spirits began to rise.

Blueberry was munching grass near the stream that coiled through the little valley. Max began to comb her down. After the chase she certainly deserved it. He talked as he brushed her round sides. "Well, girl, we have now had great adventure though not the one thought." He smiled. "You have been a fine horse and I am sorry to have led you to such a terrible ending. I suppose all our friends have been caught by now and eaten as well." He stopped brushing. "It doesn't do much good to think like that. They could be alive . . . and they could need our help. I don't think we can ever go home without knowing what has happened.

"The Duchess was right. We have let much come between us and the treasure and perhaps may never find it now. I only know that I have been so afraid that I don't think I can ever be frightened again." Tears came to his eyes as he stroked the pony's mane. "We may never get home, Blueberry, but we must follow our friends. Right now, that means . . . following the giant." When he said this Max felt as if something had been let out of him, like a cracked water cup. He felt empty and cold and alone.

"*An easy adventure is no adventure at all.*" That was what Knipper had said. A tear rolled down his dirty cheek. He wished he had never heard the word *adventure.*

And so, they set out to follow the giant. The tracks were easy to find. They were big, foot-shaped ditches, shin-deep where Willy had run. Flowers and plants in the bottom of the footprints were as flat as the pages of a book. The tracks marked the hills as far as Max could see and with each step, he began to feel that finding his friends was a hopeless plan.

"I'm afraid we haven't a prayer of finding them," Max said standing in his stirrups to gaze over a rise. He was shocked to hear a familiar voice answer him from nearby.

"There is always a prayer, good Max." It was Fanzig, sitting beneath a spruce tree. "Those who practice them, find them invaluable in such times. Kingdoms have been lost for prayers unsaid."

Max shouted for joy. "Fanzig! You are alive! That is one prayer answered already! Where are the others? Are they safe? Are we too late?"

The fox rose and Max could see from the dirt caked to his legs that he had been running very hard. "They have all been caught. I alone escaped. We thought for a time that we were safe after the giant's footsteps left us. We began to move away, but then he came upon us again. Jumpjilter tried to shoot arrows into the giant's eyes, but the monster plucked them from his brow as if they were only wasp stingers. He filled his great satchel with our flock. Jippit and Knipper he held in each hand, but I managed to get behind him and lie low in the tall grass. He seemed excited at his catch and sang a song about mutton pie and elf stew."

Max shook his head. "The elf *did* stay with the flock. That is a more noble fellow than I thought. I am sorry I ever doubted him, and it is my fault that he has been caught."

Fanzig licked a front paw. "If you thought his language was rough with *you*, you should have heard his words for the giant. I have never heard such frightening threats."

"And all for nothing," Max said, "for surely by today they have all been made the giant's dinner."

"*Today?*" The fox looked at Max. "They were taken just this morning. Have you lost memory? I see you have fallen by the bruise on your forehead — are you injured?"

"No, but I have slept so hard I thought it must be many days since the giant came. How it is that I woke so soon, I can't say."

Fanzig grinned. "It is no mystery. There is a strength in you, young Max, that would not let you rest while your friends were in danger. Come, let us go quickly, while there is time."

Max tapped Blueberry's sides with his knees, and they began to trot alongside the fox. "Do you think the giant has not had dinner already?" Max shuddered as he asked this.

The fox did not slacken his pace as he answered. "He boasted to Jippit that he would have them all for a great feast tonight. He intends to gather many herbs and roots to enhance their flavor."

"How horrible! What did Jippit say to that?" Max felt terrible thinking of the brave elf caught in the powerful hand of the giant. He knew Jumpjilter would be sure to have an answer to the boasts of the monster.

Fanzig smiled as he answered. "He shook a bit, whether with rage or fear, I could not tell. Then he laughed that mocking laugh of his. '*Ha!*' Just once, like that."

"Then we will hurry even more. We must arrive before supper time!" Max stopped Blueberry and lifted Fanzig to sit before him on the saddle, then they rode as fast as they could. The pony seemed to understand the need for haste and galloped almost as fast as she had from the giant.

CHAPTER 12

THE GIANT'S CAVE

After the first stars came out and the last rays of sunlight streaked along the hilltops, Max saw the giant's cave. They came upon it almost with no warning. That is the way of the hills of Gumbor. You may see only a little way ahead and there are many surprises.

Max sat in Blueberry's saddle listening and watching for any sign of the giant. Fanzig dropped down to stand beside them. The horse nibbled at the tall grass, ignoring the dangerous cave before them.

"I've never seen anything like it. It's as big as a castle."

"Big enough for a giant to live in," the fox agreed. "I don't like it a bit."

Max peered into the emptiness of the cave's mouth. I think I see a lightness — but I'm not sure.

"Yes," Fanzig said. "There does seem to be an unsteady flickering. There must be a fire deep inside. Shall we go in?"

Max remembered the giant's cruel face and large grabbing fingers. He closed his eyes to gather his nerve. "It would be easy to catch us in the cave. He may even be waiting for us — the fire could be a trap."

"True, all possible, but your horse doesn't seem to feel any danger and I suspect she is right. I don't have that feeling now either. Besides," the fox turned to look up at the prince, "this *is* what we've come to do, isn't it?"

Max thought of Knipper and Jippit struggling in the hands of the giant. Anger rose in him so strong he was ashamed of his fear. "Yes, that is what we are here to do. We've not come so far just to turn away. We have come for our friends and we will *not leave without them*." He said this last louder than he intended and was surprised to hear his words echo back from the cavern facing them. He turned to Fanzig. "Of course, if we can save them without fighting, so much the better."

The fox nodded. "We will use our wits, young master. Perhaps that is all it shall require."

Max slipped off Blueberry's saddle and listened as he drew his sword. Nodding to Fanzig he approached the entrance with the fox at his side. As they crept closer, the cave grew taller and wider. The moon disappeared behind its top. To Max the opening looked like a gaping mouth, ready to swallow them up with rocky, jagged teeth. He remembered terrible dreams and wondered what new horror waited here.

He felt as if some invisible hand were trying to push him away. He glanced at Fanzig and the fox's confidence in him made him determine to continue. When he turned back, he found the cave no longer a grinning mouth, but only a cave. Yes, huge and deep, but a cave and nothing more.

Past the entrance, the glimmering light grew more constant, and Max smelled the odor of burning pine. *"Let our friends live still,"* he whispered.

Moving down the great passage, they entered a large open place in the cave. It was like a giant domed kitchen, Max thought. And that is precisely what it was. The ceiling was far above their heads where an opening in the rock served as a chimney. The brightness of the giant's fire hurt their eyes. A whole tree trunk crackled in its blaze and heat washed over them in wet, sweaty smoke. Above them steam rose from a massive iron cooking pot hung by chains over the fire's pit. He feared they had come too late before a familiar taunting voice called down to them.

"You certainly took long enough getting here! Some rescuers you make!" It was Jippit Jumpjilter of course. The elf was in a wooden cage which dangled directly above them from another chain from the ceiling of the cave.

"Jippit!" Max shouted with relief. "We are not too late!"

"Nor too early." Knipper's tired voice came from the cage as well.

The sheep began to bleat from a fenced corner across the rocky floor from the fire.

Fanzig grinned up at the cage. "Master Jumpjilter, fancy meeting you here. Where, might I ask, is our host?"

The elf shouted above the noise of the excited flock. "Curse those sheep! 'Willie' is out gathering some herbs for his great feast. Imagine, trying to make an elf taste better! It shows how these giants have crude palates."

"Enough of this joking," Knipper said. "Let's be getting out if we may. I think if we wait much longer you will be joining us for supper."

Max knew the dog was right. "Let's cut through the cage. That padlock needs a key, but I don't wish to trouble Willie for it."

In an instant he was scampering up a rock ledge to stand beside the cage. Max began to hack at the thick wooden bars. After a few moments he was nearly exhausted. It was very hard wood, and his sword was getting heavier and heavier.

"Cut! Cut!" Jippit cried. "Do you call that hacking? That wouldn't pass for a good switching among the elves! Put some muscle in it! I don't want your initials carved on it, just cut it through! Hurry! Hurry!"

Max felt his muscles recoiling with shock as he swung the blade onto the hard wood. He bit his lip and kept on hacking so hard his fingers began to bleed. The cage had begun to swing around on its chain at the repeated blows.

"I'm afraid this isn't going to work," Knipper said. "I think I hear our 'Master Chef' coming home."

They stopped and listened, holding their breath. Sure enough, they could faintly hear the familiar steps in the distance. They also heard a mangled melody as the giant strolled to his kitchen.

"To home, to home,
with a good soup bone,
with the roots and bitters I have got.

"Scrubs, bark and leaves,
I takes what I please,
grinds it all and boils it in my pot!"

Hearing this, Max tried even harder, but try as he would, he could not cut through the heavy wooden bars of the prison.

Knipper looked toward the entrance of the cave. "You'd better leave now. I don't believe our host would be fond of pantry raiders."

Max was so upset he couldn't say a word.

"Come on, young master," Fanzig said and began to move down the side of the ledge.

Max took one last look at the two friends in the cage. He felt his heart would burst. "We'll find a way. Don't give up!" He had no idea what they could do but knew they must do something. He was trying not to cry out in despair as he slid down the ledge after the fox.

"Well, we're in the soup now," Jippit scowled as he watched the entrance of the cavern.

Knipper said nothing but scratched his ear with a hind paw.

Back on the floor Max glanced about the cave. "Where can we hide? There's nowhere to go." They could hear the giant walking into the entrance now, humming to himself. As he stared at the sheep Max remembered a story from childhood. "I've got it, Fanzig!" he said with a loud whisper. "We'll hide under the sheep. *Odysseus* did it to hide from the Cyclops back in olden Greece."

The fox nodded. "I don't know the story. Let's hope it was no fairy tale."

The boy and the fox went to the flock. Though the sheep knew them well, they had a hard time getting them to stand still as they crawled beneath them. Max had to hold the leg of two rams to keep them from bucking away. Fanzig held the leg of a very frightened lamb firmly in his mouth. They had to hold on very tight as Willie entered the room.

"Well, well, well!" the giant bellowed. "You have decided to stay for supper then?" He laughed at his joke. "Ah, now I have everything I need for tonight's feast. I'll just put it all in the pot and let it boil for a spell, then in you go."

"For a great cook, you certainly don't know anything about selecting your dishes." Jippit Jumpjilter scorned.

"What? How dare you say that! But what do you mean, my little elf pudding?" The giant leaned down to hear Jippit's answer.

Jippit smirked. "Oh, everyone knows that elf does *not* go with dog, and you certainly *can't* be planning to serve either with sheep — never. It's simply not done. Crude. Crude — even for a giant."

"Poor Jippit!" Max thought. *"He's stalling for time. But what good will it do? Sooner or later Willie will grab the sheep and we'll all be cooked!"* He shuddered and tried not to cough from the wool pressed in his face.

The giant laughed again. "Ha! Ha! You try to upset me, little man! What would you know of such dishes? How many elves have you eaten? Now be quiet, I have searched long and hard for the herbs and mushrooms I shall use, and I am tired. I am not in the mood for your jests."

"Nothing relaxes an elf like pestering a giant," Jippit said. "I am always amazed that so large a beast has such a small brain."

Without warning, Willie roared at the top of his voice and the cave shook so hard that rocks fell from the ceiling. After this there was only the sound of the scared sheep. All else was silent.

Willie glared. "Now, be quiet! I tire of you. If you must make noise, then sing Willie a song. A gentle song so I may rest. All you elves sing pretty, it comes natural to you."

"I'll sing nothing to you, you . . ." Jippit stammered.

"You sing or I stretch your ears from here to there!" the giant snarled and started toward the cage.

Jippit could not help clapping his hands to his ears. Then he began. "I will sing a song about the wind and the willow tree. You must understand that in elfin tradition we say that the wind is in love with the willow. It is the saddest tree when the day is still, but on a windy day it comes alive."

Willie sat down with his back against the cave wall. He uncorked a giant-sized wine jug and poured out a cup as large as a barrel. "Yes, a very pretty story, sing the pretty song."

Jippit cleared his throat and began. His voice was not perhaps beautiful, but Max had to admit it was clear and full of feeling. It was truly not a sound he would have expected from Jumpjilter.

"Said the wind to the willow as he blew one day,
'I've come to court you from far away-
over the oceans of the world I roam,
I'm in the white-tops, playing the foam,
but there is no place the wind calls home."

As Jippit sang, the giant took a long drink of the strong wine that Max could smell across the room.

"Mountain peaks and valleys deep,
In the middle day where eagles sweep,
Full round the lonely world, I speed,
Nowhere do I find my heart's need,
I return at last, truly freed."

Max saw that Willie's eyes had closed and his head was nodding slowly with the soft tune.

"Roll and bowl and tilt and twirl,
the trees in the wind all over the world.
They all tremble and make great spree,
there's none so graceful as the willow tree,
That is the song that the wind sang me."

The last words of the song were drowned out by the snoring giant who lay still with his head against his shoulder. Max let go of his sheep and stood up.

CHAPTER 13

THE GIANT'S SUPPER

For a long tense moment Max stood watching the dozing giant without moving. Taking a breath, he began to move across the stone floor, one careful step at a time. None of the captives dared say a word as Max came near the snoring Willie. He felt cold as he stood so close to the powerful arms and strong, clutching fingers. He studied the key which was tied in loose fashion to the ogre's belt. It was tiny in Willie's hand but almost as long as Max's forearm. It would be hard to lift. He swallowed and crept closer to Willie's side. The giant's snoring was rough and uneven. Max could feel its breath as he reached a hand to the large knot holding the key. He began to pull and push at the knot, working to unravel it bit by bit. One hard push could wake Willie and he would be caught without hope. The knot seemed to take forever and then, without warning, fell apart. The heavy key, free of its hold, slid from the belt and clanged on the rock floor before Max could grasp it. He froze then lifted his gaze to the giant's face. He was staring directly into an enormous open yellow eye. He could not speak. He stood rigid, waiting.

"*What* have we here?" Willie snorted. "A side dish of boy! The meal grows tastier every moment. I'll make sure there is a place for you, little friend. You led me a pretty chase this morning. I'll bet your horse is here-abouts as well. This is the finest bit of luck Willie's had in a long, long time. Greybeard and Ole Rainey can't snub their noses at me now. Not with the fine table Willie sets." Chuckling, the giant clasped Max in his hand and sat up. He sniffed the smoky air. "The stew spices smell near done. I'll just take this sword," he said, pulling the blade from Max's helpless arms, "and let you swim! I hope you've washed lately — I don't like my food too dirty."

Max was petrified as Willie held him out over the boiling pot. Then he heard Fanzig's voice.

"A riddle, giant. A riddle as large as you. Will you hear it?"

Willie turned his head to see the fox strolling up from the sheep. Knipper and Jippit stared in horror and Max shouted, "No! No! Run, Fanzig! He'll eat you too!"

"Another supper guest," bellowed the giant. "I'm not sure I have *room* in my pot."

Fanzig continued. "You giants are supposed to be the

masters of riddles. It is said to be tradition among you that you must answer a guest's riddle before dining. Of course, that is just custom among the nobler giants of royal blood, so I doubt you'll pause for it. I'm afraid it would be too difficult for you anyway. Go ahead, feast. But you'll never hear my riddle."

Willie threw back his head and laughed. "I have never had a supper refuse to be cooked! Go on with your riddle. I shall not cook you until I answer it, but that shall be hardly another moment."

With that, Fanzig began his riddle very calmly. If he were nervous, he did not show it, but that is the way it is with foxes.

"When it's cold, I drop in, but then you complain-
When it's hot I rise to go, but then it's the same.
When it's nice and summer, I like to boast,
for then I leave and run to the coast . . . who am I?"

The giant listened in silence and then began to grin and smiled his crooked smile. His ugly teeth gleamed yellow green in the firelight. "That is indeed a good riddle, master fox! One that cost me a dinner once, a long while ago. But I learned its answer. You are the *rain*. You drop in when it's cold and rise in clouds of steam when the sun shines. You run down the river to the sea and the coast. Ha! Ha! And now you will join us for supper as well."

Max could hear Jippit groan. He was thinking as fast as he could and as he stared at the dancing fire below him, he had an idea. He shouted at the giant as Willie once again held him over the pot.

"I know a riddle you can never guess in a hundred years! Not if you guessed all day and night for a hundred years! Cook me and you lose it forever!"

The giant shook his head. "I know all the riddles. I've heard every one. You can't trick Willie, you know."

Max shouted desperately, "You haven't heard this one!" *And that was true, for he was just then making it up.*

Willie sucked his cheek and smiled. "All right, but you are only to live until I may solve it. My, but what fun we are having tonight."

Max fought down his nerves and cleared his throat. He tried to put his idea into the proper words of a riddle.

"You may run all day, but you'll never get away!
I match you easily . . .stride for stride . . .
When I wish, I am taller—
though sometimes I am smaller . . ."

Max stammered for a moment, hunting for a way to put his thoughts, but found his rhyme just before Willie could complain.

"All day long, I need not hide!
All your muscle and all your strength . . ."

Again he searched for the words.
"You can't harm me at . . . at any length! Who am I?"

There was a long quiet pause when Max finished speaking. The giant began to work his mouth around, then to rub his hand across his brow. "Bigger?" he grunted. "Nobody's bigger than Willie, but Greybeard . . . but I'm faster than he is."

Max shouted, "Much bigger! Much bigger!"

The giant snarled and set Max down as he began to pace back and forth across the room. He grumbled as he walked. "I can beat *anyone*! No other giant can beat Willie, except maybe Ole Rainey, but he's not as tall."

"You can't harm me a bit!" Max yelled. "Not even a little bit!"

The giant stamped a foot and roared. The room shook so hard the fence around the sheep fell down and the poor lambs huddled together bleating miserably. Scowling, Willie tramped out of the cave.

"Quick! The key!" Jippit shouted.

Max was already running after it. The giant had not picked it up from where it had dropped. The key was very heavy, but with Fanzig holding the thick twine with his teeth, they dragged it across the dusty floor. Getting it up the ledge was even more difficult, and Max had to stop to catch his breath and get a better grip. Every moment he expected Willie to come romping back. He was afraid even to think how soon the giant might guess the answer.

At last Max had the key at the cage door. With shouts from Jippit and barks from Knipper, he managed to fit it into the lock which was as big as a cheese wheel at the palace. Jippit reached through the bars to help hold it and together they twisted the metal bar as hard as they could. Just when it seemed that it must be the wrong key, the lock swung open and fell from the cage. With a cheer Max jerked the door open and steadied the hanging prison as Jippit and Knipper leapt onto the narrow ledge.

The prince felt his heart beating so hard he thought at first it might be the returning steps of the giant. With all that they had been through, their escape seemed almost too easy. Derek had warned him that things that seem too easy, usually were. He knew they must not rest until they were far from the giant's lair.

CHAPTER 14

THE WAY AHEAD

It seemed to take forever to get all of the sheep out of the warm cavern and into the darkness outside. Every moment they expected to hear the tread of the giant's return. Max was happy to find Blueberry had waited near and came at his call. Out of the cave the four friends faced a new problem.

"Which way to go now?" Knipper asked. "We came closed up in Willie's great bag. I have no idea where we are, or which way to the mountains."

Max looked to Jippit. "You wouldn't know the way back to the elf road, would you?"

Jumpjilter dug his hands into his pockets. "My grandfather was never caught by giants. As Knipper said, I'm afraid I couldn't see which way Willie traveled to bring us to his cave. I only know one way through Gumbor, and it might be in any direction from here."

Fanzig looked into the night sky. "If the clouds would part a bit we could at least tell north from south."

The other three looked up when Fanzig said this. A few stars were visible, but not enough to name them or to chart their direction. In a small corner of the sky the moon stared back at them like a round blank face, confused as they were.

"The mountains are to the south of Gumbor, but where is south?" Knipper drew his jowls into a pucker as he sought some way to choose their course.

"With or without a path, we must go somewhere, and soon," Jippit said. "That overgrown ogre will stumble over us in the dark if we just stand around agreeing we're lost!"

Max was thinking. He remembered something Derek had told him. "Isn't there a steady wind that blows here almost every night?" he asked.

Fanzig turned to look at Max as he answered. "Yes, there is the North Wind, but the hills and valleys make it wind around so that you cannot tell its true direction."

Max turned back to the giant's cave. "Would you say the cave is in the highest hill we have seen?"

Jippit answered. "Of course, but what is that to us? We could not see the mountains from it, even if it were high enough, not until daybreak anyway."

Max grinned. He knew his idea was right. "Jippit, can you see the smoke?" he asked. "The smoke from the giant's kitchen comes out of the hill and rises to meet the North Wind. If we can follow the smoke, we will be traveling south — to the mountains."

Jippit watched the smoke for a moment and began to laugh.

Everyone cheered Max and began herding the flock away from the cave, following the smoke. This was fine for quite some time, but then in the darkness the smoke thinned away. They continued to travel, trying to keep to the same direction but after an hour they found their own tracks. They changed direction but again they came across their old path. They were making one large circle after another. Tired and upset, they lay down to sleep. They made no fire for fear that the giant might see it. It was another miserable night in the hills of Gumbor.

When the grey morning came, the travelers remembered how hungry they were. The sheep had plenty of grass, but the four friends had gone without food too long. Max divided the very last of his dried beef but this was not much better than going without. "It only reminds one of food." Jippit said.

They were all in poor spirits and did not say much to each other. Still, Max could not help asking where they would be if they had not had to leave the road to Dimbarrel's farm.

Knipper shook his head. "We'd be there tomorrow night," he answered, "but if we'd gone on to the bridge, we'd be in our graves right now." Knipper saw how disappointed Max was. "We are alive, and free again. There's that to remember."

Max sighed. "Dimbarrel's farm. And then I would be going back after the treasure."

Fanzig sat next to Max. "It is not good to think so much of what might have happened, young Max. There is only one way a person can be certain of — the one he travels. I see you are tired of my advice. We are all tired. But let yesterday be. There are enough things to worry with today."

"True enough," Jumpjilter said, licking the last shreds of dry beef from his fingers. "And a fine dreary day it appears to be. Just right for worrying, I would think."

Max had to laugh. Some things were constant, he thought. *The sun rises and the elf complains*. It was good to laugh. He couldn't remember the last time. Then his tense stomach rumbled, and everyone joined his laughter.

"Well," Jippit said, "we are not the *only* ones in Gumbor with rumbling bellies this morning. I am surprised we haven't heard the echo of Willie's stomach. That would be a noise indeed."

Max thought of the giant. If Gerald could have seen him in the cave, he could no longer think him such a baby. He enjoyed the laughter of these friends — not family or servants, but friends who shared danger and adventure, who trusted their lives to each other.

After the meager breakfast, Max climbed the nearest hill to scan the horizon. The early mist was thinning away. At first, he thought the day might be near as grim as the night. Then his eyes grew wide as he saw the thing that they had searched in vain all night to find. Ahead, the hills rose and swelled into sharper green slopes, hardly hills at all. And behind them, tall and jagged, pressing into the sky like wide axe blades slicing from the earth, stood the mighty Runruggel Mountains. Long flat clouds seemed pinned to the peaks, streaming out like flags trailing in the wind. As Max watched, the sun broke over the clouds and yellow rays splashed across the cold heights. The peaks burst into flames of light, glinting red and shimmering gold in the brilliant daybreak. It was the most beautiful thing he had ever seen. It might even be the most beautiful thing there was. For several minutes Max stood alone watching, not saying a word. When he called to the others, they joined him watching the sunrise together with new hope of freedom.

Trying to describe it later, Max said it was like hearing a wonderful hymn in a great high church though there was no sound at all. The mountains made troubles seem small. In fact, everyone felt much better. Max thought of his brothers and hoped they had avoided misfortune on their journeys. No doubt they were nearing the treasures the Duchess had marked out to them. He wondered at the tales they would have to tell him, but at this moment, he did not envy them at all. Encouraged, the prince and his party rounded up the flock and set off directly for the mountains.

***

Derek

Derek had not come upon much traffic on the road north of Low Arden, until cresting a hill he met a line of peasants walking south. Men pushed wheeled carts packed with jugs of water, small barrels of meal, grain, or grease. There was here and there an item of crude furniture such as a stool or table. One cart was pulled by a donkey and an old woman rode in it with several small children. The men and women walked quietly in this train. All looked dirty and downtrodden. These were no serfs headed for a fair or market. They looked to be refugees of war. He pulled off the path and slipped down from the saddle as the first of them came past him. As the donkey-drawn wagon rolled near, he stepped forward and raised a hand in greeting. A youth walking alongside, pulled the harness, stopping the wagon.

"Pardon me, good mother," Derek said, bowing in courtly fashion to the old woman perched above him. "Might I speak with you a moment?"

The youth turned to look at the old woman who nodded to him. She smiled at Derek. "As you wish, sire. We have little, but if you need a drink of water, Efren here will fetch it for you."

Derek shook his head. "Nay, ma'am. I wish to ask what plight has put you on the road?"

The woman closed her eyes and patted the head of the little child seated next to her. "We were the village of Kurn, sire. A month ago, it was, we welcomed our new young Earl. He came to take up the place of his father. We rejoiced with merry making, but something went very wrong." She placed her hands over the ears of the resting child. "The dragon comes. All shrieks and blasting fire. Like as in old times . . . first time since I was a wee girl, like this child. That time the dragon only killed the cattle and burned the chapel down. It was told that the earl made a bargain with the dragon and no more would he come. Not 'till now. Now it's all burned up. Not a house left standing. No place for us to live . . . we're on our way south and hope someone will have us."

Derek swallowed. It occurred to him that this great adventure was a lot more important than his quest for a prize; to these people, it was survival. He motioned to Moonstone who stepped near and pulled the bag of money from his saddle. He slipped a few coins into his tunic then held the bag up to the woman. "Here is a small bag of gold coins, but they will see you all to Gaspaar and treated fairly when you arrive. Tell a warder that Prince Derek sent you and will ask an accounting later."

The band of peasants all bowed to the prince and a

woman behind the cart sobbed and leaned against her husband. Derek tried to smile but waved and climbed back up on Moonstone and rode swiftly past the quiet band. His heart burned with anger at the cruelty of the monster.

***

Gerald

"So, my Prince, Master Gorna speaks well of you," the Duchess said. "You have learned more rapidly than any other pupil. Is it not so, Gorna?"

Gerald saw the wizard nod though he did not speak. The Duchess lifted something from the fold of her cape — a golden chalice decorated with designs he had seen carved on the walls of the chamber.

"Perhaps, you are now ready for another taste from the fountain? This drink is from much nearer the source."

Gerald had been disappointed at the taste of his first drink, yet he had set his mind to the training of Gorna and indeed felt his senses attaching themselves to the simple spells he was learning to construct. He took the offered chalice. To show reluctance would be unwise. Might it be another test? There was a strange aftertaste. Now he realized he saw more clearly the size and shapes around him in the cavern. The candles seemed much brighter. Beside the Duchess and Gorna appeared two cloaked figures. These silent ones wore hoods and their eyes were not visible even in the new light.

Gerald spoke. "So, my Lady, you have other pupils here as well? I did not see them before the candles flared."

The Duchess chuckled. "The *candles* are no brighter my Prince, only your eyes are more *open.* These have been here all along. Everything you learn here is about seeing more

107

and more. There is *so* much to see! *Few* are those who see it."

Gerald nodded. "It is said that appearances are deceiving."

"Perception is an art. To appear a thing others desire or fear, carries a price. One must be careful in the use of such skills. The deep arts change one. You cannot turn back if you travel far on this path. For certain ones the power grows easier to control. What a gift for a *king* to have! Do you begin to understand?"

Gerald swallowed the last of the drink. He felt as if he had had too much wine, but instead of feeling sleepy, he felt he need never sleep again. The lady's voice seemed far away but clear. Everything since he had come down the well seemed a dream. *No*, he thought, everything *before* he came down the well seemed a dream. "Yes, I understand. There is a price to pay for becoming a rightful ruler. Is the fear of this what makes others think it evil?"

The lady laughed. "Ah, you *do* understand! Good and evil — right and wrong — those are words for the weak ones, the ones who need leading. True knowledge is beyond such simple words. The wise must rule the weak. It is what must be . . . for *balance*."

CHAPTER 15

THE LOST WAY

Max and his band traveled most of the next two days in high spirits. Jippit said he didn't think Willie would answer the riddle any time soon. "Perhaps less than your *hundred years,* but he'll likely find another meal before it and that'll be the end of thinking of us! I think his belly and his mind are closely connected."

Every time they topped a hill, they could see the mountains, and each time they were a little closer. That made the journey easier. Finding a fresh stream, Jippit brought out his hook and line and they enjoyed a tasty fish dinner. The hard hills of Gumbor changed. Now among the long grasses and scraggly spruce trees there was a berry bush here and there. "The roots run deeper now," Jippit said when they met oaks. Marching along, the elf darted off and brought a wild onion and turnip he had seen on their path.

"Mother Earth sets an ample table, young Max," Jippit grinned. "But good manners for this meal are a keen eye, a strong arm, and a slight taste for grit."

The prince began to think they could bring the flock home to the shepherd's farm after all. There might yet be time to find his treasure. On the third morning, Max asked, "How much farther? The hills are steeper, and there are so many trees now."

"In perhaps two days we might see the farm," Knipper answered. "I have never entered the mountains from this way. It is hard to be sure."

Max counted the days of his journey. He had left the castle on the first day of May. That was nine days ago and as yet, he had not gone a step after his intended treasure. Still, there was time. There must be. He began to sing a song the maid had taught him as he rode but kept forgetting the words. Something about knights riding up a hill and down again.

"You call that singing?" Jippit grinned. "I shall sing you a song for travelers!" He threw back his head and sang an elf song that cheered everyone. He sang much better for his friends than for Willie.

*"Far beyond the mountains, through the olden doors,
the golden road rolls homeward, to the mystic shores!*

*"Now my feet are happy with stepping of the way,
each step draws me closer, day by brighter day!*

*"Laughing grasses, singing water, tinkling bells, cheer me
home!
I'll lay down my walking rod, from here I'll never roam!*

*"Come out, sisters, come out brothers, sing the welcome
song!
I am coming Elfenland, I have been too long!"*

The day was growing old when all their happy thoughts
and songs were brought to a sudden end. A familiar, dreaded,
echo rose, far behind them. They waited, listening. There was
no doubt of it. It was the giant.

"Run!" Max shouted. The whole party rushed in the way
they had learned to in these dangerous hills. The poor sheep
knew the giant's sound as well and hurried with no pushing
from Knipper or Fanzig. Jippit swung onto Blueberry behind
Max and held on tight as they bounced over the rolling hills.

They were at the very lap of the mountains and yet
there was little hope of escaping the giant. Max fought the
terrible feeling in the pit of his stomach. It was so unfair. With
freedom so close, would they be dragged back to the giant's
kitchen? Was all their running for nothing? Max knew the
speed of the giant, but he knew they must try. They must not
give up. He shouted encouragement to Blueberry as she
struggled to carry her riders the winding way between the hills.

The terrible voice rose in the distance. Not yet loud but
very clear.

"Willie knows the answer! Willie knows! Who is taller than Willie? Not Greybeard! Who can Willie never hurt? Not Rainey! Willie knows! Willie knows! *Shadow! Shadow!* Willie's shadow!"

Jippit groaned. "It took him *three days* to figure it out and he has the *nerve* to be proud! Oh, to be caught by such a tiresome enemy."

Max leaned forward to look for any shelter as they turned a bend alongside a narrow creek. "There!" he shouted. "Some kind of road!"

"Fat lot of good it does us now!" Jippit shouted back.

"We shall run faster on level ground!" Knipper yelped from behind them.

"Yes!" Max answered, but thought, *'So can the giant.'*

The sheep poured onto the worn dirt road. They did move faster and Blueberry as well. Max was thinking of a new plan when they turned the next bend. They came at once upon a large band of men standing across the road.

Max started to shout a greeting, but his cheer froze in his throat. He recognized the leader of the band. Here was the wicked thief who had tried to rob him and nearly killed Knipper so many days ago. He saw the others were a rough-looking sort as well. Each held weapons: staffs or axes, and several had bows and arrows.

"Robbers!" Max shouted the warning, but it was too late. They were already upon them.

"Halt!" the chief cried. They had little choice as the men drew their bows.

"Well, well! We meet again, lad," the leader said as he rubbed his bandaged hand. When he grinned, Max saw he had lost some teeth and the prince thought how much like a live scarecrow he looked.

Knipper turned to Fanzig. "We have come a long way

out of our way to meet these fellows anyway. All roads lead to trouble it seems."

The fox pricked up his ears. "But we have brought a *new* friend to meet them, as well!" he whispered.

"I'll just have your sword there, boy," the bandit said as he swaggered toward Max. But he stopped in mid-stride and came no closer.

The earth began to shake, and the outlaws looked to each other, puzzled and frightened.

With an ear-splitting yell Willie bounded over the last hill and landed with a shattering impact beside them, gouging two foot-deep craters beneath him. He carried a boulder as big as a wagon and raised it above his head to hurl.

Seeing the thieves frozen in astonishment, Max spurred Blueberry off the road into a gully. He shouted for the others to follow as his brave horse crashed through the bramble and thorns.

Willie gave another ringing battle cry on finding himself among the villains who were quick to shoot their arrows with no effect at the towering giant. Enraged, he threw the huge rock at the scattering band. He was too excited at the sudden confrontation with this desperately violent pack of robbers to think of the boy and his sheep following their shepherd in his dash into the brush. The last Max saw of Willie over his shoulder, the giant was busy stuffing handfuls of fleeing outlaws into his great sack.

Max and Jippit clung tight to Blueberry as she galloped fast and wild through the heavy brush. The gully was longer and steeper than Max expected, and they seemed to be falling as much as riding. He hoped that Knipper and the flock could keep up. As the sounds of the battle behind them faded, Blueberry stumbled on a vine. Her riders were thrown high and headlong into the thorns and thistles. Down they tumbled.

Max closed his eyes for fear of the sharp thorns. The fall seemed to take much longer than he thought it should. He hit and rolled and rolled. When Max stopped, he opened his eyes but saw only darkness. He reached to feel his eyes in fear. For an instant he wondered if he had died and was already buried in his grave. Then he heard Knipper's voice and sighed with relief.

"Be patient, my friends," Knipper called from high above. "We shall find a way to get you out."

Then another voice replied from much nearer Max in the dark. "No point in that," Jippit Jumpjilter said. "Better to find your own way down here instead. The Elf-Road will take us into the mountains."

CHAPTER 16

INSIDE THE MOUNTAINS

Max felt his way in the dark tunnel into which he had fallen. Was there no end to the things that could happen on an adventure, he wondered? "Jippit, are you near me?" He called. The prince jumped when he felt a hand on his shoulder.

"Quite near, really," Jumpjilter chuckled. "I suggest we begin to help the others down."

Max shook his head. "I suggest we get some torches first. I can't see a bit."

The elf laughed. "I forgot you Tall Ones see so poorly! Let's go up, then."

Climbing out was easier than Max feared. He held onto Jippit's cloak and followed just behind. Jumpjilter found a carved stairway made up of shallow but very wide steps. Max realized it would not be difficult to lead Blueberry or the sheep down them.

Returning into the fading daylight, their friends greeted them with smiles of relief.

"I thought you had broken your necks," Knipper said. "Blueberry neighed like murder when she tripped. She is lucky not to have broken a leg. You really should be more mindful of your horse, young Prince."

Fanzig gazed down into the black hole in the tangle of vines. "So, this is the elf road again?"

Jumpjilter answered as he began to hunt low tree limbs for torches. "Certainly. You don't think I would lead you into a strange cavern, do you? I follow the road handed down—"

"From father to son — yes, I know," Fanzig went on. "It's just that I've never thought of elves as being great ones for tunneling. A short-cut under a river perhaps, but a passage beneath the mountains? It hardly seems elfish."

"Well . . . "Jippit began, "it's not, strictly speaking, an elf tunnel."

"What?" Max looked up from feeling Blueberry's ankles. "Then why are we to follow it?"

Jippit scowled. "The elves use the tunnel; they did not build it. The dwarves dug it long ago before a great war. They abandoned it when the war ended. There's no gold in it, so they have quite forgotten it. It is a convenient route for the elves, and I must admit, it seems a well-built tunnel. Dwarves are the masters of such things."

"Then there are indeed things in which an elf may be

outdone?" Knipper barked heartily.

"Oh, there are a few folks better with a shovel, I suppose," Jippit answered.

A sudden thought occurred to Max. "What of water? We have many sheep, a horse and all of us of course. We don't know how long we shall journey until we meet more, do we?"

Knipper nodded. "A concern, yes, but sheep can go many days without water. I would worry more about forage for them."

Jippit nodded. "As I recall the stories, the dwarves built cisterns at their guard posts and forts within the tunnels. Yes, and tended mushrooms in their caves to supply their sentries. Might that nourish a sheep?"

Knipper frowned. "For a time. I should not wish it alone for many days, but it would pass better than nothing."

Max looked back on the hillsides. "Well, we can gather up a lot of grasses and bind them in our packs, Jippit and on Blueberry's back, but I do worry at water for her."

Jippit nodded. "I think we must trust the dwarf-work cisterns to have lasted. They'd have been fed by rainwater draining through air crannies in the rock no doubt. Dwarves are quite meticulous when it comes to life beneath the earth."

Deciding this was their best chance, Jippit worked to make up a great supply of torches for the days they must march in darkness, while Max cut long grasses with his sword and stuffed it into their empty packs and rolled a large amount inside his sleeping roll to tie across the pony's back. They stuffed what turnips and berries they could find in her saddle bags along with the last of her oats. Despite their preparations, they knew the next few days would test them. Knipper let the flock graze long on the grasses nearby to fatten them up for the treacherous underground road. It was near morning when Max set the first torch ablaze and followed Jippit back down the narrow steps. The sheep had no problem with the stairs, but Blueberry was skittish. Max had to coax her with gentle words as he led her to the cavern's stone floor.

The tunnel was surely well made as Jippit had said. It was the first true dwarf work that Max had ever seen. He was amazed at how precisely the hard rock had been cut. The floor felt smooth as a royal courtyard. After they journeyed many hours through the passage they came on a great opening in the tunnel. Another natural cavern joined their own. The walls and ceiling almost disappeared in the vast wideness they entered. Their torch light sparkled on wet rock sickles hanging from the high roof above them. These sickles were matched by mounded columns below climbing slowly to join them through the centuries. They paused to study the wider way. Max could hear only the echo of water dripping in the dark stillness. It was hard to stand long here listening.

"This is 'Rottog Grameer'," Jippit said. "The Caves of Time. The Dwarves discovered them while digging the mountain tunnel. Legend tells that many of them wandered off into the darkness and were never seen again. I suggest we stick to the smooth-cut path."

Max nodded and they went on. They were all glad, after ages of walking, to pass from the deep blackness of Rottog Grameer. It was a relief to find the hard walls of rock narrowing back to surround them again. They were also happy to discover a lengthy spread of mushrooms along the sides of this new passage. The untended crop still grew here even if no dwarves remained.

They noticed strange marks cut into the walls now and again. Max asked Jippit if he knew what they meant. The elf frowned. "Distance markers of some sort, I suppose, though I would have expected a number instead of runes."

Fanzig interrupted. "Perhaps I may be of help here. I know something of the language of mountain dwarves."

"I thought they had all vanished," Max said.

"And so, they have to most eyes," the fox replied.

Jippit hated to admit his ignorance but his curiosity was greater than his pride. "What do you read, then?"

"They tell the name of the mountain above us." When Fanzig said this, everyone stood still, and a long silence rolled over them in the coldness of the passage. "We have come from the hills and are now beneath 'Megwill Ladiwol'. She is not one of the rocky ones, but far greater than a common hill."

Knipper nodded and began to speak in a strange way, as if reciting something he had learned long ago:

"*Megwill Ladiwol, green shawl shoulders with soft aspen hair, comforts the stranger who wanders there.*"

The dog turned to the others. "I know this mountain well. Her leaves are the first to tell of spring. You can see her from Dimbarrel's farm."

The others were happy to hear this news. Thinking of the tons of rock above them was not so scary now.

They had all grown weary on their long march beneath the earth and decided to make their camp for the night. Though the cook had packed two tallow candles, he thought it best to save them. In the dark after he smothered the torch light, Max could feel a slight draft.

"Yes," Jippit said from nearby, "the dwarves' channels for fresh air. Good work to last so long."

"How long?" Max whispered.

"At least two hundred years," the elf said and went to sleep.

Max tried to imagine dwarves digging out the great passage under the mountains, but horrible thoughts of Rottog Grameer and the poor lost creatures in its depths came to his mind. He pulled his blanket near his chin and closed his eyes. The only sounds he could hear were Blueberry's snores echoing down the tunnel.

***

Randrew & Maeve

Queen Maeve stepped onto the balcony of the palace of Gaspaar. She had awakened at a dream and had seen that King Randrew was not in bed. Pulling on her robe Maeve moved to stand beside her husband.

"What wakes you, Randrew?" she asked. "Do you feel pain? Shall I send for the physician?"

"Not tonight, dear Maeve, only such troubles as a dream may bring. Did I wake you?"

"Nay, it was also a dream which woke me."

"Let us hope it is not the same dream, for mine was frightening enough for two."

The queen frowned. "I saw Gerald in peril, in a dark green place, though I knew not how. He smiled, and I was troubled by the smile more than anything else I could think."

"A smile may mean many things. A dream may mean nothing."

"And your dream?"

"Aye, Max also rests in darkness, but an echo dripped, like soft footsteps, and things moved that I could not see. Steady black eyes — like a dog's — kept watch, and I felt no fear of them. What does that mean if anything at all?"

Maeve took his arm. "It means we care for our children and must pray for their journeys."

The king turned to look at his wife. "Was I wrong to send them on this quest, Maeve? Was I a bad father to demand such a challenge now? Such a hard test especially for my youngest son?"

120

The queen took a deep breath. "You faced danger at his age when even the very young manned the walls against the Viking raiders. That was not your father's wish also. The physician's hard warning of your health and future days is much the same. You must make your choice before you would wish. You have required only a search for what is great in the land. It is your sons who will make of that what they will. They are not your sons for nothing, Randrew. It is only strange we have not dreamed of Derek."

The king laughed. "I pity the nightmare that meets that lad! It won't last long enough to wake either of us."

CHAPTER 17

WHAT WAITS AHEAD

Max was not sure why he was awake. He did not know what had waked him or how long he had slept. Deciding he had had a nightmare, he turned on his side and closed his eyes again.

It made no difference. In the mountain tunnel, without a torch, the darkness was the same with his eyes open or shut. Then he heard it. Very soft. The tread of feet or paws on the stone floor. Something was there. It was not moving now, but it was there in the dark. Standing. Watching. Waiting.

Max slid his hand until his fingertips touched the hilt of his sword beside him on the floor. Clenching his teeth, he strained to hear any sound. His arm ached. Sweat beaded his cheeks. And all the time his eyes stared at nothing but darkness. He could stand it no longer. He sprung from the floor, sword in hand, shouting. "Stand! Stand, whoever you are!"

All the others jerked awake and the sheep started their noisy bleating. In the confusion Max lost any idea of where the intruder was.

"What in the Magician's Hill are you yelling at?" Jippit Jumpjilter shouted, rubbing his eyes.

"A torch would help matters," Fanzig said in a worried voice.

Max fumbled for a bundle of branches as Knipper tried to calm the sheep down. Jippit lit the torch quickly with a flint and turned to face Max. "Now where is your enemy?"

Max stared down the tunnel past the light of the torch which hurt his eyes after the deep darkness. "There was someone . . . or something, here," he said. "It was watching us. I think it could see me very well in the dark."

"Like an elf?" Fanzig asked.

"An elf would have seen *me* and not been afraid to stay," Jippit objected. "It seems our hero has had a bad dream."

"No. It was not a dream, or an elf," Max declared. "It seemed like — well, like something sort of thick and heavy — and mean. It just didn't seem like an elf."

"I'm certain there have been mean elves," Fanzig said, "but I doubt if there have been many heavy ones."

Jippit was about to reply when Knipper called to them from further up the tunnel. He had his nose to the floor. "Something has been *here*."

They all went to join the dog.

"I smell the fresh scent of something with hairy feet. It also carries a pouch of foul smoking leaf with it. There are bits of the stuff on the floor," Knipper said, studying the stones.

"*I wonder . . .*" Jippit mumbled. His eyebrows scrunched together.

"Whatever it was, it seems to be afraid of us," Max offered. He hoped this was so.

"It might prove wise for one of us to stand guard while the others rest," Fanzig advised.

Knipper agreed. "I shall be the first. It is a role I am used to. This strong smell of pipe leaf will keep me awake anyway."

"I will light one of my candles," Max said. "This is a time for it, I think."

With this they all went back to sleep except for the dog who settled down facing the long tunnel ahead of them.

Hours later, as they again traveled the tunnel, Max spoke with Jippit about their mysterious visitor. "I wonder if it might be one of the robbers from back at the road. One could have stumbled into this tunnel before we found it."

"No, no, the elf answered. "I think the outlaws spent most of last night trying to 'out-riddle' Willie. Besides, the brush covering the tunnel entrance was not crushed before we fell — that is, before we *entered* the tunnel."

Max held his laughter. The elf's pride would never admit to having stumbled onto this trail again by accident. The prince was certain Jumpjilter would only relate how he had led them step by step in any elf tale that might be later passed down.

Jippit continued. "Anyway, I believe I know what our guest was last night."

"What?"

"I'm not entirely certain," Jippit answered, "and won't guess. Elves don't jump to hasty answers. We leave that to you Tall Ones."

Max knew that was all he would get out of Jippit about that, but there was more he wanted to ask the elf. He had been curious about the speaking beasts ever since he had met Knipper and Fanzig. "Jippit, truly Knipper and Fanzig are the most amazing creatures I could ever have imagined, yet I know nothing of how they came to be in Gaspaar. They are the greatest of friends . . ." he shook his head. "Yet they are not like anyone I have ever met. They seem to be part man and part beast, but really like neither. I only know I like them both and they seem to know something of everything."

The elf was silent as they walked along. Presently he answered. "You are right to say they are not like people, Max, for they are not. They are not of men, but the helpers of men — or so the legend has it. Still, they are friends in a very true way."

"Please, explain this to me," Max asked.

The elf sighed. "Well, it's all legend of course, and you may take it or leave it for all I care. The *speaking beasts* were given to the people of this land many years ago as helpers. They are as the beasts were before man learned to steal and kill and waste things. Of course, they didn't speak before, but man learned many good things from them and was better for their help. These beasts speak, for this is the way man learns now. But they may be the last."

Max shook his head. "Who gave them to the people of Gaspaar?"

Jippit frowned. "Legend again, of course, but if you must hear it . . . "

"Yes, of course, I must."

Jippit continued as they walked. "The Queen of Izmah is supposed to have done it because Gaspaar's people were the wisest and kindest of the lands. Their king Todd tried very hard to follow the right way. The beasts who spoke were to help them."

"King Todd!" Max said in a loud whisper. "He was my great-something grandfather. But who was this Queen of Izmah?"

"Really, Max, you ask far too many questions." Jumpjilter's tone was stern, but Max could tell he enjoyed telling this tale. "Legend on top of legend. Izmah was a magic kingdom in the clouds ruled by a wise and beautiful queen. Some called her an angel. If you put much trust in that kind of tale most people will think you are quite a fool."

Max grinned. "Most people would think me a fool to believe in elves."

Jippit grunted and looked ahead past the torch light.

Max knew he had gotten all the answers Jippit would give just now. Well, there would be time for more questions later. Now they must find the shepherd's farm.

The travelers had paused to study another dwarf-marking on the tunnel wall. Fanzig sat down and blinked.

"I'm afraid my eyes are tired from this torchlight, good friends. It is hard to read this sign, but as best I can tell, it speaks of '*Lidill Torrinth*'."

Knipper nodded. "The Baby's Tooth. The first rocky slope of the Runruggel Mountains. Not so big as the great 'teeth' ahead."

"How far to Dimbarrel's farm?" Max asked.

I don't know the way of this tunnel," Knipper answered, "but Lidill Torrinth is but a day's march from Dimbarrel's valley."

Max beamed. "Only a day!"

"But every bit of a hard day's journey in this tunnel," Jippit said. "I'll have a good rest before we begin."

The others agreed, though they had found no more mushrooms and a single small cistern was cracked and almost dry though Blueberry was slow to abandon the last wet remains of its shallow bottom. So, they set their camp again beneath the mountains, but finished the first tallow candle and began the other before as they took turns watching. They did not forget their 'visitor' of the night before.

CHAPTER 18

A HIDDEN ENEMY

They were hungry now and having found no more mushrooms, they had used the last of the gathered grasses from their packs to give the sheep a mouthful. They were all eager to leave the tunnel. Max had emptied out the last of the water from his leather flask into Jippit's frying pan for the fox and dog to lap up. They left what little remained for the lambs, but it was hardly enough.

"They'll have all the water they can drink soon," Jippit said as they walked along. "The tunnel should fork ahead, and your road will open into a valley."

"Our road?" Max questioned. "Do you mean you are leaving us?"

"Our roads have been the same since the Willtil, good Max, but soon the way to Elfenland shall change its course. My road shall be the other fork of the tunnel."

Max was saddened to think of seeing his new friend go, but was glad they would be leaving the tunnel soon. "Wouldn't you like to rest for a day or two at Dimbarrel's farm?"

Jippit shook his head. "There will be time to rest in Elfenland." The elf paused a moment before speaking. "Know that you are an elf-friend, Prince Max. Few Tall Ones have been able to claim that."

Max nodded but could say nothing.

Knipper came up to them. "Our friend, the hairy footed smoker of foul leaf, has been here just before us. Fanzig wants to search the tunnel ahead before we bring the flock through."

The fox trotted up beside them. With your permission of course, good Max."

Max looked down the dark passage. "I think we should stay together until we come out of the tunnel. Jippit says it will be soon." It seemed odd to him that Fanzig asked his permission. He had not thought of himself as their leader, but with Jippit leaving, he knew the others viewed him in this way.

The hours dragged on now. Praying the tunnel should soon end made the deep darkness troublesome. They were hungry and thirsty. Max remembered the water he bathed in at home with no thought of it.

Fanzig called from ahead. He waited at a large archway in the left wall of the tunnel. A frilly dwarf sign was carved above it. Everyone came to stop at the entrance and peered into the blackness beyond the arch. "There is something about '*Karzad Keep*' and a warning to enter at your own peril," the fox said.

Jippit raised an eyebrow. "Quite right. The dwarves set deadly traps in tunnels that lead to forts or castles. I shall need be careful."

"Is it safe for you to go in then?" Max hoped the elf would change his mind.

Knipper sat down. "Here's some more news. Our 'mysterious visitor' has been here also. He has traveled this other tunnel it seems. Whether coming or going, I cannot say."

Fanzig was looking up their passage. "Perhaps he waits to see which fork we will take. Perhaps he watches even now."

They looked down both tunnels and then at each other.

Jippit broke the silence. "Prince Max, it has been a true and noble adventure to travel with your party. May you find a great treasure and rule Gaspaar for an age. Peace and Wisdom!"

The elf was speaking loudly, Max thought. Perhaps elves spoke in such a way when bidding farewells. He knew none of their customs.

Jumpjilter turned to the two speaking beasts. "Knipper, old shepherd, watch over your blighted sheep. Their company I shall not miss. But you have a calm most elf-like. That is a compliment few have heard. Keep your head and use it." He turned to the fox.

"Fanzig, guide Max as I would do. Be ready for all as an elf would. Farewell, I leave for Elfenland and home!" With this he shook Max's hand and strode under the dark archway.

In a moment he was gone from their sight.

Max could hardly speak. Even with his two good friends beside him, he felt alone. He stood still until Blueberry nudged his shoulders. "All right, girl, I know. You are thirsty! So am I. We head now to Dimbarrel's farm. But keep an eye for any dark shapes ahead." He palmed his sword hilt. He shrank from the thought of using it. Real fighting was not what practice with Derek had been.

An hour later Max's torch burned out. As he fumbled to find another one, Fanzig laughed.

"You won't need to strike a torch, my Prince, we can see well enough now!"

Max looked up. "Yes, we can see. It's light! And it's bouncing all over the roof!"

Knipper wagged his tail. "I hear water rushing ahead."

Blueberry neighed and brushed past everyone.

"Blueberry smells it!" Max shouted.

They all ran. The sheep moved in a white swarm toward the sound of crashing water growing louder and louder. They heard Blueberry's loud galloping ahead of them toward the new brightness. Max licked his lips realizing how thirsty he was. The walls and floor were flickering with bright greens and blues. Rounding a bend, they came to the end of the tunnel.

Blueberry danced in a round circle of flashing blue-green light. A waterfall rumbled down just outside the mouth of the tunnel. The sunlight, pouring through its current, colored the walls, roof, and floor in a swirl of cool brilliance. To one side of the tunnel a rocky ledge had been carved out leading around the fall. There was a little pool just inside the tunnel mouth and Blueberry was splashing in it, the water sloshing white around her knees. The sheep scampered ahead, pushing, and butting to reach the pool and the pockets of still water that collected among the rocks that they could lap up.

Max cried for joy but could not hear himself for the loud crashing of the falls. He raced to the pool and lay on his stomach to take a long cold drink. In a few moments he pulled off his boots and rolled up his britches and joined Blueberry in a lark. At the edge of the tunnel, he stretched out his hands into the falling torrent and scooped back a mouthful of the cold mountain shower. He had never felt so fresh and alive.

Splashing about, kicking water at Blueberry, Max decided to have a look outside the tunnel. Fanzig and Knipper were following the ledge around the falls, heading out into the sunlight, but Max grabbed a tight hold on a boulder and carefully leaned his head into the falling water. The heavy shower pounding his neck and shoulders made him shiver, but poking his head through the blue curtain, he saw it was worth the cold.

The falls rolled down far below and pounded into a pool of churning mists. A large stream pushed out from the pool and wandered through the valley below in sweeping bends and rounded loops. The valley was a wide V-shape, its meadows and pastures running smoothly up the sides. Their bright green was speckled with the yellows and reds of mountain flowers. Trees grew so thick atop the valley walls they seemed almost a hedge to mark its boundaries.

Knipper and Fanzig were just to his left standing on the rocky path that led down to the valley below. The dog barked in surprise to see Max's face appear in the wall of water and Fanzig laughed heartily.

Something hard and rough grabbed Max's arms. Had he been inside the tunnel he would have heard Blueberry's warning. One moment he was struggling to grip the boulder and the next he was being shoved out over the thundering falls.

CHAPTER 19

MAX AND DEREK WONDER

Everything swirled about Max in brilliant colors. A glint of silver flashed as his sword flitted away from his scabbard. The world tumbled. One instant blue sky above, the next, the foaming pool below. His heart froze but he drew into a tight ball of arms and legs and clamped his eyes shut. There was a loud hard slap as he struck the water. He did not open his eyes until he bumped on the sandy bottom of the pool.

Even with the blurred vision of being underwater Max could see the surface above splintered in a thousand dancing mirrors. He pushed up with burning lungs wondering at his survival. His back stung where he hit the water but there was no sharp pain from broken bones. A great column of white bubbles cascaded down where the force of the waterfall struck the pool. Bubbles flared out and floated up in glittering clouds like an upside-down fountain in a palace.

Breaking the surface, he could hear Knipper barking through the thunder of the falls. It was loud here on the surface, but below, the roar had been so great Max was hardly aware of it. He looked up at the height he had fallen from high above the pool. He shuddered. Someone or something had tried to kill him. He was more than lucky to have missed the rocks. Shaken and soaked, he climbed out onto a grassy bank. His teeth began to chatter, and he could not make them stop for a time.

"Max! Max! By Izmah, Fanzig! He is alive!" Max saw the dog loping down the twisting path.

When his friends reached him and heard what had happened, Knipper shook his head. "It shows how we must always be careful not to let down our guard. This was the work of our strange visitor in the tunnel, I would guess. It is a small wonder that we have not lost all for our folly."

Max knew the real folly had been his own, playing tricks at the waterfall. "I hope we can at least find my sword. I have no idea where it landed, but it . . . it might be needed sometime." Nodding at this request his friends spread out along the edges of the pond to search. The prince was relieved when Fanzig soon shouted to him.

"It is here, Max! You are fortunate not to have lost it. A few inches less and it would be completely gone."

Max hurried to look where the fox pointed with his

snout. The sword stood stuck in the shallows of the pool. Only the hilt and a bit of the blade were above the water, standing up like a small silver cross. Max waded into the water and pulled out the blade that glittered wet in the sunshine. Something about this felt familiar, as if he had done it before, or perhaps dreamed it. "Why does this feel so strange to me, Fanzig?" he said. "It feels serious. Like a kind of omen."

"You would not be the first king to draw his sword from the water, young Max." The fox was still looking in the pool where the sword had stood, as if there were something else to see. But there was nothing.

***

Derek

"Yes, master knight, this is the land of Empt, and empty it soon will be." The old peasant shook his head as he spoke to the prince astride his charger. "Smart ones dare not raise their families here and serfs slip away. No one likes living in the shadow, but the truth is, we older ones had grown used to it. This time the terror is too much and even I have given up my own home in Kurn and am journeying south. My master bid me tend his fields, but Gorackle burned them down."

"Has your master released you from your vows of fealty?" Derek took the drink the old man handed up to him on his saddle.

The peasant laughed. "The new earl broke his word and did not keep the dragon's bargain. He did not send gold or silver, or even a piglet to the forest at new moon. I know, for I have carried the ransom for the old earl many a year. A master who breaks his bargain is stripped of his title. I no longer am his vassal to command."

"Well, I suppose some good may come from any

137

misfortune. Why did your master not meet his bargain?"

The peasant shrugged. "He is young and raised far away. When his father died and he returned to take charge of the land, he did not believe the stories. 'Superstition,' he called it. I tried to explain it to him, but he said he would not believe a *tale* of a dragon until he saw a dragon's *tail* for himself." The old man laughed. "Well, seeing's believing, and now he's been schooled!"

Derek passed down the water jug. "You say you carried out the bargain for your old earl? How was this done?"

The peasant frowned. "I'd take the gold or silver or, if it was a sparse time, a piglet or two or a brace of chickens. There's a big stone table in the heart of forest Quist. A place no man should see if he is not paid to. I'd leave the bargain on the stone and be off. Only once did I stay hid to see if t'was a real thing or some outlaw's trick. Never saw, nor ever heard, the like of it! All *wing*, all *claw*, all *teeth*, all *eye*. That's as good a look as I can give you and more than you'll ever want to see."

Derek nodded. "I want to see him all *dead*. And I mean to. How far is Kurn?"

The peasant grinned. "My, my, the eager knight ain't you? Do this trick, my young lord, and they'll sing a song of you. You're two days from Kurn. With all the burned-up cattle, I think they'll be more than willing to share charred pig and cow with any who happen by. No doubt it will be tough and dry by your arrival."

Derek pulled a gold coin from his tunic. "For your trouble, your tale, and your water, grandfather. Good fortune to you in the south. I am from Gaspaar and better land it is for company and comfort than this. Show that to a warder and say Prince Derek gave it to you."

The journey had been longer than Derek had thought.

He had never been this far to the northwest though tales of the northward dragons had been in stories and games when he was a child. Could it be true that this "Gorackle," as the Duchess named it, was the very same one about which such children's tales were told? He remembered a snatch of a song from his mother's maid.

"Keep your babies, quiet old man -
No fires at night outside.
There sleeps a dragon in the land -
Quiet children keep their hides."

Derek whistled the old rhyme, then stopped. "That's probably good advice tonight, Moonstone. We'll put out our campfire at dusk and sleep in the shade. The land here is strange, and though it does not burn, the tooth seems to be warmer. That old worm may be sleeping somewhere in those distant hills."

***

Max

Max breathed in the strong wild smell of the open valley. Walking in the broad sunshine again was delightful. The tall grass all but covered the sheep, burrowing through it like so many great white moles. Blueberry was in high spirits, bucking and rushing ahead, then running back right past them shaking her mane. Max did not ride her now. He felt she had shared burdens enough in the dark tunnel. His clothes dried in the sunshine as he walked barefoot through the cool grass with his boots hung on Blueberry's saddle. He was tempted to sing Jippit's elf song but knew he could not do it justice.

Fanzig looked over at the shepherd's dog as they

walked. "Your valley is more lovely than even I had hoped, Knipper. Everything here seems happy to be growing."

"It will do, I suppose," Knipper replied in his usual calm tone, but Fanzig could tell he was quite proud. They were old friends. "Only one man has touched it," Knipper continued, "and Dimbarrel is a shepherd. He understands caring for things and working with the land and not against it. The growing things are happy here."

"I hope Dimbarrel is feeling better," Max said as he walked beside the two friends.

"He is a sturdy oak. He is old and gnarled, but his roots reach deep," Knipper smiled. "He will be back before we expect, if I know him."

"That is good. These sheep need a true shepherd," said Max. "I have run them ragged, I'm afraid. They are just skin and bones now."

The dog looked up at the boy. "Yes, they are skin and bones now, but every bone is here safe and sound. You have risked your life and a kingdom for Dimbarrel and his sheep. There have been few shepherds that cared for their flocks as you have cared for his."

"Knipper speaks truly, Max," Fanzig said. "Your adventure has been a finer sort than most. It is a quest taken for someone else, someone in need."

Knipper stopped and turned to face them. "We are here," he said. "This is Dimbarrel's farm."

All about them the meadows spread out in flowing waves of green. Ahead on a small rise stood a pine cabin. The doors and window shutters were a sky blue and there were flower beds against each wall. A rainbow of wildflowers tumbled from them.

The sheep seemed to know they were home and moved to fill the yard about the house and barn. The young lambs jumped and ran for a time before settling down to eating the grasses. Max could see they were glad to be done with traveling.

"So, my adventure ends," he whispered.

CHAPTER 20

THE SPY IS FOUND

That evening they set about to prepare a proper supper. Dimbarrel kept several hens and Knipper was sent to round them up. Finding the hens was not too difficult but discovering their eggs was not so easy. They had been turned loose to feed while the shepherd was away and many of them had nested in the strangest places. Max discovered two eggs on the roof near the chimney and could never figure out how the hen had managed to settle there. Later he pulled a large pitch-sealed barrel from the stream which contained packed cheese kept fresh by the cold mountain water. He was pleased to find turnips, carrots, and onions in a garden behind the house and Fanzig topped off their bounty by bringing in several bunches of wild blueberries. It was the finest meal they had had together.

After the feast, Max leaned back in the shepherd's rocking chair. *What must I do now?* he wondered. He had completed his task for the shepherd and though much time had passed, he was free to pursue the quest his father had set for his sons. The map in his boot showed a trail east from the inn, but the inn was far from here. It was hard to believe he might still find the tree with no color and, if he managed to reach it, return in time to present it to the king on the last day of May. He admitted he had indeed let "beasts and burdens stand in his way" despite the Duchess' warning. Perhaps he had lost his chance, but he determined to finish his quest because he had taken it, no matter how it might end. He must rise early in the morning and set off again with no more sulking. If he claimed to be his father's son, he would see it out. He felt a sort of peace settle on him with this promise and knew he would enjoy at least one good night's rest without worrying. He was too tired to worry.

As Max was just dozing off from the long day's journey and the large supper, there was a sudden loud scuffling outside. He recognized a familiar voice and sprang to his feet. Knipper and Fanzig were beside him when the door burst open and the cause of the commotion stood before them.

Jippit Jumpjilter had a tight grip on a strange little man. The point of the elf's knife was under the captive's chin. Jippit grinned. "Here's your *Tunnel Rat*," he said, shoving his prisoner into the room.

The little man was just shorter than Jippit, but much heavier. He smelled of the strong pipe leaf and his glare was so fierce that Max jumped back though he saw his hands were tied.

Max recognized him at once. "This dwarf is the Duchess' servant! I saw him at the inn."

"That's right, lad," the dwarf said. "You'd been better off to have taken her advice than to be taking up with these circus animals!"

"That's enough of your lip, Hairy Toes." Jippit poked the dwarf with his dagger.

Fanzig turned to Max. "Are you certain this dwarf was with the lady you spoke of, Max?"

"Yes, I'm sure," Max said. "He knocked me down."

"That's very odd indeed," the fox continued. "For this is Scrugnit, a servant to the Witch of the Runruggel Mountains."

Max stared at the fox. "Are you sure of that?"

"Well, well, fox," the dwarf 's voice was an ugly snarl. "you've come a long way to poke your snout into her Wickedness' affairs. Remember you're not in your cursed forest now. These are *her* mountains."

Max gulped. "Do you mean the *Duchess* is the Witch of the Runruggel Mountains?" He shuddered when he said this, thinking of how close he had been with her and never even guessed.

The dwarf laughed an evil laugh.

Knipper ignored Scrugnit. "It seems a good thing you've come so far out of your way, after all. If you had followed her plans, there is little doubt there would have been evil done."

Max closed his eyes and sighed with relief. He had no idea of the witch's plans but was glad these beasts and burdens had blocked his way after all.

"I think it would be wise if we discussed just what was that treasure the *Duchess* sent you after, Max." Fanzig twitched his snout. "I imagine we should learn much from that."

"Yes!" Max was more than glad to tell them all now. He only wished he had done so much sooner.

"What about our friend, Scrugnit, here?" Knipper nodded at the dwarf.

"We should slit his gizzard the same way he'd do us." Jippit said.

Scrugnit swallowed hard. "You won't hear much from me if you cut my throat!"

"He's right," Max said. "We'll keep him tied up." He could not allow Jippit to harm the dwarf. Scrugnit was their prisoner now and in their charge. Knights don't do such things, Derek had told him, and it sounded right.

After this, Jippit tied Scrugnit in the chicken coop and the friends all sat down at Dimbarrel's table. Jippit explained how he'd said his farewell in the tunnel so that their enemy would lose track of him. He planned to overtake them from behind and catch the villain by surprise. When he learned of Max's fall, he was furious. "If I had known the thief pushed you, Max, I'd have brought him back stiff as a stake."

Max was still amazed at the deceitful Duchess. "I can't understand how we all believed her," he said.

"Don't be too upset, Max," said Fanzig. "It is an old trick. A little beauty hides a lot of evil. I am afraid few look far beyond a pleasing face. Besides, this witch has powers to cast enchanting spells. She lulled you and your brothers into believing you each knew a secret. People like to believe secrets they are told. It makes them feel important."

Max nodded. "You are right about that. I felt so important about my secret that I didn't even share it with you, my most trusted friends."

Jippit leaned forward. "Well, come on then! I've been wondering all along about that. What *is* this great treasure?"

Max spread the secret map out on the table. "The Duchess — I mean the *witch*, told me a magic tree grew in a forest of gold and silver to the east. The tree is so bright it has no color and if I were to cut it down and take it to Father, the whole palace would be filled with wonderful magic, just like the forest." Max noticed as he spoke that his friends were staring at him with wide eyes and open mouths. Knipper let out a low growl.

Fanzig explained. "There is indeed such a tree. Did she tell you why she has never cut it herself?"

"I meant to ask her that," Max said. "I, I just couldn't seem to say anything. Everything I wanted to ask seemed silly to me then."

"She cannot enter the forest," Fanzig continued, "because there is a spell to keep her out. Those with truly evil hearts may never enter."

"But why?" Max asked. "What magic is it that is so important? Why should the witch wish for me to cut down the tree at all?"

Fanzig looked to Knipper and nodded. "I will tell you, young Max," he said. "It is an old story, and not ended yet."

***

The Duchess

The lady the brothers had known as the "Duchess"

settled an elbow on the long table at the head of the dark hall. Bracing her arm, she cradled her chin in her open palm and looked past the man who sat next to her at the table. "I have decided to lay a lordly knight on the plate of your dragon, Gorna. A bold prince, gone strutting forth in the wilds."

The balding wizard beside her brought his hands together before him, intertwining his fingers. The long nails gleamed in the green glow of the deep chamber. "My, the lands seem full of princes of late. Yet, such a favor, my lady, without even *asking*? Dare I hope it might also help thee in some fashion?" His eyes narrowed in a crafty smile.

The Witch of the Runruggel Mountains slid her eyes to her companion but else-wise did not move. "None that could not be helped in other ways, though I should like to spend my time in other courses. I make you a gift that will please you, for in this bait I have laid a hook that belonged to you once which I held in payment for another day of deeds."

Gorna blinked. His eyes narrowed. "Do you speak of..." He paused, as if to calm himself. "Surely, you would not release old debts for a trivial matter among such friends as you and I?"

The lady did not change her expression and Gorna dropped his eyes. She spoke. "Yes, I speak of your missing tooth, Gorna. And a mighty spell I have placed upon it. Not an easy spell to build or cast. If you will hear my request, much may be profit to you and I and all who serve the Green Fire."

The wizard nodded, keeping his eyes on the lady. "Speak it. For you have called the council here and before others arrive, I would have our business understood between us."

The lady held three fingers up. "There are three brothers who seek a treasure to claim the crown of their father when he dies. One is your pupil, Gerald, who sees himself a cunning mind, a rich *mine* indeed for us to quarry. He shall become a choice puppet. He learns quickly and this shall make him useful sooner than I might have hoped. I shall let him think he thinks for himself. He is a foolish tool whom pride can rule, but a weapon which must be handled with care to be used at a better time."

The wizard waited for the lady to continue.

"Another who I shall give you is Prince Derek, a brave fool who wishes no more than a good clean fight. A high-minded knight on a noble quest. The easiest prey of all."

"So, my fool is the *easy* prey? A brave knight I'll warrant, with an arm of steel no doubt. You offer my horned head readily enough. Perhaps you wish him to succeed and narrow the circle round the Green Fire?"

"Nay old friend," the lady cooed. "For the fool wears your tooth around his neck. It warms when you are near and when you kindle your dragon's fire, it glows hot beside his skin. Yet, you have the stronger warning for you will sense him at every turn and daylight or dark, you'll know his heart beats just behind that echo of your smile. He cannot hide as long as he follows his secret guide to you."

The wizard grinned. "You said there were three."

"Yes, I did, didn't I? There is the one . . .Max, the youngest prince. An innocent and simple lad. His end is certain, but he may perhaps deliver the most return of all. His way leads to a place long forbidden us. In following his quest, he may do that one thing that we cannot. And much would end… and for us — *begin*."

Gorna chuckled. "You wear the black ring well, my lady. Well indeed."

CHAPTER 21

FANZIG'S STORY

Max and Jippit looked at each other before settling back to listen to Fanzig's story. Now he would get some answers, Max thought. Waiting for Fanzig to begin, he noticed the fox's eyes seemed to be staring somewhere beyond the shepherd's cabin. When he spoke, he hardly seemed to be speaking to them, but reciting a tale passed down through countless winters. One that had not been heard by men for many years.

"Long ago," Fanzig began, "when King Todd had freed the dwarves from a very wicked ruler and peace was full in the land, the Queen of Izmah came to Gaspaar. She called the king into a magic mist which hung near the castle. The king, thinking he knew his way quite well, entered at the lady's bidding. When he had done so, he found himself, not in a mist, but standing in the heart of a great forest far from his castle. The king knew he was in the presence of a mystery beyond his understanding and turned to the lady to await her words."

Though Fanzig told the tale, the words hardly seemed to come from him at all.

"'Lord Todd,' the queen said, 'since the days of the world's beginning man has lost and forgotten much, he was given. He has lost the very garden where he was born — a garden much like this one, filled with such fruit that would refresh even his spirit. Such things would taste bitter to him now, for he has lost the taste for them. This is the sadness of man — that he has tasted of hate and greed and murder, so that the taste of truth is bitter to him now. See how all the world thrives on such things.'

"King Todd bowed his head when he heard this for he knew that it was true. He had just fought a great war and had seen the wickedness that men may do to each other. But his eyes brightened at the words the Lady spoke then.

"'Yet still man may hunger for the truths he has known. For though they are not the way of the world he has conquered, he knows that love and mercy and justice are the good things he needs. That he must have to be full. Those who know this have chosen a hard way, for the powers of evil and pride are strong in this world. But to those that choose to search for these true things, they are worth the dangers.'"

Max was leaning forward in his chair. It was hard for

him to understand it all, but just hearing of these things made him tremble with excitement. They were nobler than anything he had ever heard.

The fox continued with the queen's words. "'Because you and your people have chosen this hard way in the world, I have the joy of giving to you a long-lost gift. The first friend to man — the beasts of the field and the fowl of the air.'

"Then King Todd knelt down, for he knew the Queen of Izmah was a great lady. 'Dearest Queen,' he said, 'forgive my simpleness, but we have long had the beasts of the field and the fowl of the air. We shear them for our clothes and milk them for our drink. We plow our fields with them and even hunt them for our table. How may you give us what we already have?'

Max looked around at the others and saw that they were all listening to Fanzig with great care. Jippit Jumpjilter had even forgotten to eat the hot bread he had taken for his supper. It lay cooling in his plate. Max turned back to Fanzig, who continued.

"The queen looked down at the king and smiled. 'When the world was new, man was the keeper of all things, and all things served him well. But when he lost the good things he had known, all that had been in his keeping was changed. Man is no longer as he was before, and neither are the beasts as they were. No more may the lamb lie down beside the lion. Still, the beasts stayed close to their master and still they served him. As you say, they give up their coats for your warmth and even their lives for your food. In all this have the people learned the lesson of their giving?'

"The king bowed his head again, for he knew that the people had taken these things with little thought or thanking.

"The queen spoke again, 'Now there shall come to your land, beasts as they were at the world's beginning. Their great pleasure is to serve you as did all things once. Man learned much from the beasts before, but now he is so blind that he must learn in a different manner. These new beasts shall speak to you in your own tongue. Do not be frightened of this but learn. For the beasts may often see men in a way they cannot see themselves. Think not that they are as men or as demons. They are beasts . . . the lost friend to man.'"

Max licked his lips which were quite dry and listened hard as Fanzig continued the story.

"'Remember, O King, though these beasts are wonderful, it is for man that they came to be. Man alone of all creatures is the chooser. Of this may come good or evil. Yet this is his purpose, to choose, of himself, for the right — or for the wrong.'

"The queen held out her hand to the trembling king and in it was a little twig. 'Take this seedling,' she said, 'and plant it in this forest, which is the heart of Gaspaar. So long as it grows, the speaking beasts shall befriend the people of Gaspaar. Yet the people may lose these friends by turning back to selfish ways. Still, until a child of your family line plucks up this tree, at least a few such beasts shall walk your forests and hills. And no matter how few they are, the land shall be the better for it. Remember. The day this tree is cut, much good will leave Gaspaar until the end times.'

"Then King Todd took the seedling from the lady and planted it in the warm soil. Tears came to his eyes at the strong words the lady had spoken. He turned and called to her. 'Dearest Queen, I beg you! When I am grown old and this is forgotten . . .what then? What hope is there for the kings of evil times to come?'

"The Queen of Izmah turned to the king and answered, 'Truth becomes neither young nor old, my lord. Those who truly seek it are of one generation though a thousand years stand between them.' With these words she left him.

"When King Todd at last looked back at the little tree he saw that it was changed. The sprout began to blaze like a fire but did not burn. So brightly it shown that the king could not see its color. 'It is a color with no name, for it is not for man to name it,' he told his wife when he returned home. King Todd lived long and had many children and there was a good peace in Gaspaar."

After Fanzig had finished speaking there was silence as everyone considered the tale.

When he spoke, Max's throat was very dry. "You mean I — I could have ended you — you and Knipper — by just plucking . . ." the terrible thought of the witch's plan made the words catch in his throat.

"I thought it was all just legend," Jippit began. "Now I understand that it has been passed down from father to son. We elves stand by such tales."

"Not all legends are false," Knipper said. "Now you know about us, good Max. You also see just how wicked this Witch of the Runruggel Mountains is. She is very clever and has nearly caused you to begin a great evil without even knowing it. I am afraid that the times now are much worse than in old King Todd's days."

Max closed his eyes. "Yes, it is much sadder in the land than I had ever known. Since I have left the palace, I have met robbers and witches and wicked giants and evil dwarves. It is no wonder there are so few speaking beasts left. Even the innkeeper warned me that I could not trust people as I traveled the land. Why? What can be done? Can things ever be made right again?"

Fanzig looked at Max until their eyes met. "Do you really wish to know what is to be done?"

"More than anything," Max answered. "This evil in

Gaspaar seems greater to me every day. It seems I have been running or hiding or talking in secrets since I left the castle. I would do anything to bring back happiness to the kingdom."

Knipper studied Max before he spoke. "What might be done, might very well be hard. It might be harder than anything you have known before."

Max looked at the faces around the table. They had treated him as a true prince and now they were asking him if he really wished to be one. He thought of all he'd seen on the journey. The evil giant and the robbers came to mind. He remembered the innkeeper's warning that folks could not be trusted with another man's sheep and to keep his gold hidden from other travelers. Looking about the shepherd's simple cabin, he saw how little this good man really had and thought of all the gold in his palace at home. Here was Jippit, an elf leaving the land because of hatred for thoughtless nobles. And Fanzig and Knipper — were these to be the last of the speaking beasts? Max felt a great heaviness inside him for he knew that all these things were very wrong. They demanded a true hero. There was a cold whisper in his heart. *You are not enough.* He was no hero. He would fail them, and all would be lost. His chest burned with shame. Yet he knew he could not turn from this question.

"I am not enough. I cannot do this alone. Yet I would face anything to free Gaspaar of these dark times."

Jippit Jumpjilter jumped to his feet and said in a very solemn voice, "Then you *are* King to Jumpjilter! I am your servant in the adventure that comes."

Max was shocked and a little embarrassed to hear Jippit say such things. "I am no king," he said. "But you are my friends always."

The elf nodded and sat down, but he did not smile.

"Perhaps we are going too fast now," Knipper said.

"One thing at a time. For every day, there is a way, remember. Let's worry with the worries at hand."

Max swallowed and grinned. "You are right, Knipper. My head spins with all these thoughts of changing the land. What do I know of such things?"

Fanzig raised his snout. "You are learning, Max. You have learned that things are not always as they seem, and that you know less than you believed you did. That is quite a lot in so short a time."

"What shall we do with the dwarf?" Max asked, happy to be turning his thinking back to their nearest problems.

"I can get him to tell us where the witch is now." Jippit played with his dagger. "His tongue would loosen plenty if I were to tickle him a bit with old 'snick' here."

Max shook his head. "If we did such things, we would be no better than the robbers."

Fanzig agreed. "Max is right there, Master Jippit. Still, I wonder what we should do now? Max no longer has even a treasure to hunt."

Knipper scratched his ear with a hind paw. "Well . . . if it's treasure we are after now . . . I know someone who might help."

"Who?" the others all asked at once.

Knipper blinked. He enjoyed their curiosity and having an answer to Max's problem. "There is an owl not far from here that knows all kinds of things," he said. "Old Fletcher would know where a treasure or two would be, I imagine. The only trouble is, that he has forgotten more than most folks know. It takes him a while to remember things. He is older than any other creature I have met."

Jippit jumped up again. "He will remember if I shake his feathers a bit!"

Max laughed. "You are so ready to help others find their

tongues, good Jippit. I thought elves didn't care much for loose talkers?"

The elf scowled in his old manner and sat down. "After a week with these bleating sheep I merely wish to hear a clear and thoughtful word!"

They all laughed at this.

CHAPTER 22

THE WITCH'S TREASURE

Sleeping in the shepherd's big feather bed was a great pleasure that night. Only a few days before, Max would have thought it a crude and rough pallet. After all the nights he had his blanket on the ground, it now seemed more wonderful than any mattress in the kingdom.

He awoke to a rooster's crowing and the crackle of eggs frying in the kitchen. Max stretched and turned in the bed to look out the window. The mountains were a dim purple in the day's first light. What a good life this must be, he thought — a home in the mountains with a nice flock of sheep and a great friend like Knipper. What worries could a shepherd have? Just as he thought this, his eyes fell on a wolf's skull mounted above the bedroom door. The sharp white teeth were clamped in a menacing snarl. Max frowned. He had never thought of shepherds as brave before. *There is always something for even a shepherd to face*, he thought. Dimbarrel must be a brave man.

The door opened and Jippit Jumpjilter came in wiping his hands with a towel. "Breakfast is ready, Max. I thought you might rest a little longer after going over the waterfall yesterday."

"Yesterday?" Max asked. "It's funny, Jippit, things seem so long ago. I feel like I've been on this adventure all my life, and two weeks ago I didn't know any of you! But I'm fine, Jippit, really."

The elf nodded. "Knipper says it won't be easy to wake the owl. The old bird sleeps when the sun shines, you know."

Max sat up from the bed. "I guess that's right. Still, I wish we could —"

"I told Knipper you couldn't wait a day for a silly old owl's beauty sleep if you were to be king," Jippit continued. "We're leaving as soon as he and Fanzig return."

"Where are they now?"

"Checking to see if there is any sign of wolves in the valley. It is unusual this time of year, Knipper says, but if he is to leave the sheep and lead us to Fletcher, he needs to be certain."

Max tucked his hands behind his neck and leaned back on the headboard. "It's good to have them here, isn't it, Jippit? The sheep, I mean. It's good to have finished it. It's something done 'all the way' as Father says."

The elf raised his eyebrows and clicked his tongue. "Yes, yes, of course," he said. "I'm certainly glad to be rid of the little nuisances. Now we may travel with some true speed.

And we must if you are to win the crown."

"King or not, Jippit, I am glad to have met you."

Jippit did not say anything for a moment. "There'll be time to be glad or sad when this business is done. If we had all been a giant's sandwich the other night, I suspect I would not have cared that I was eaten in good company."

Max shook his head. "What shall we do with Scrugnit?" he asked, changing the subject.

Jippit huffed. "I should say we must either do away with him or keep him a prisoner with us wherever we go. The chicken coop won't hold him for long. Of course, the best thing to do would be to give him back to the dwarf king. He'd know what to do with Scrugnit, all right. Yes sir, those dwarves know the way to straighten out a 'crook'. It's just a shame it's so far to their realm."

Max didn't care for the idea of keeping Scrugnit near them either but could not see fit to 'do away with him' as Jippit said. "I guess we'll have to put up with him, then."

Jippit nodded. "As you like it."

He didn't like it at all but said nothing as Jippit left the room. Max began dressing for the day's journey.

After they had finished breakfast, Max and Jippit went out to feed the dwarf. They found he had not become more friendly overnight.

"Well, well, well, if it isn't the boy who would be king and his midget friend. Send the lad for a treasure and he comes back with a pack of smelly sheep. Heh! Heh!" Scrugnit snickered.

"I could teach you to make sport of elves," Jippit said through clinched teeth.

"You are a fine one to talk so brave with me tied hand and foot. Untie me and we'll see if elves are more than talk," the dwarf smirked.

Jippit laughed. "We are more than fools also. Just wait until your own good king gets hold of you. You'll wish you were back in the comfort of this chicken coop, I'll wager."

The dwarf's face went a chalky white and the crooked grin disappeared. He turned to Max. "You — you wouldn't send me to Darien, would you? Not really?"

"Who is Darien?" Max asked.

"The dwarf king," Jippit answered, "and a fine one for justice, I am certain. It would be a great journey, but I should enjoy every step."

"Please!" Scrugnit turned to Max. "I beg you, Good Max, have mercy. I am but a slave of the witch. I have only done what I was forced to do. Punish me if you wish, jail me, yes — but by all those fine things you speak of, don't send me to Darien!"

Max was amazed at the dwarf's words and even more by the terror that covered the man's face. He had not seen such fear before. It seemed to change the proud Scrugnit into a whimpering beggar. The dwarf was a broken man, no longer hateful, but only pitiful. He wondered if the witch had worked this change in the sad creature. Maybe Scrugnit had not always been such a vile one. Max spoke. "If you will do as we tell you and not try to escape, if you help us — then, perhaps —"

"Anything!" the dwarf broke in. "Of course, I'll help. Don't doubt it. On the road in these lands you'll be glad of me. No, no, you won't need to worry about *Scrugnit* anymore!"

Jippit looked at Max and nodded to the doorway. When they were outside, he spoke. "That's a sad one all right. Not much man left in him, I guess. Still, he's dangerous, Max. I wouldn't trust him outside our sight for an instant. If he's so quick to help us now, he'll be quick to ruin us later if there's a way."

Max took a deep breath. "I think you are right, Jippit. We cannot trust him far, but if we are careful, maybe he will help us just enough."

Knipper and Fanzig trotted up.

"Shall we begin?" the dog asked.

"Yes," answered Max. "We will bring Scrugnit with us. I don't like it, but I don't like leaving him here alone either."

"Quite right," Fanzig agreed. "Let us mind he has a blindfold and is tied at all times. One lax moment and the dwarf will be gone."

Knipper blinked calmly as he added, "And the witch would know where you are quickly enough then, Max. I think she would find you a little too near her for comfort."

Max did not understand. "What do you mean, near her?"

"She is the Witch of the Runruggel Mountains, good Max," Fanzig said. "These are those mountains, are they not? You have drawn closer and closer to her ever since you left the inn. That was not her plan. She knows that you have not cut the tree, for she would have sensed it. She does not know where you are now, or else she would be here. She must be occupied elsewhere and perhaps she has not felt your approach to her realm. As long as we have her dwarf, she may not find out."

With that last thought they fetched Blueberry, blindfolded Scrugnit, and left the valley.

The way Knipper led them was south. When they came to the wall of the valley, Max wondered how they would get through the thick growth of dense underbrush. It looked as dark as night under the trees. Max was amazed to see Knipper enter a space between two pines that seemed not to have been there at all a moment ago. Now they were on a winding path that he would never have seen. It was so narrow

they had to walk one after the other in a single file. Max had
to get off Blueberry, the branches were so low. As they walked
in the cool dark shadows, they could see the road made many
forks. It was like a large maze — not a good place to be lost.

After some time, they came out of the tight path and
the thick forest. They had left the valley. The day was starting
to cloud over. The cool breeze in the open ground felt good to
Max after the stillness of the forest. It was much easier to
travel without the sheep. They were soon far from the thick
woods and climbing a steep ridge skirting a very large hill.

Knipper paused, sniffed the air, and dashed into a
thicket of pine trees on their left. Almost a minute passed
before he returned and motioned the others to follow.

Being careful to keep a hand on Scrugnit, Max and
Jippit left the road. Fanzig and Blueberry followed. The horse
nudged Max in the back as they went into the trees.

The ground began to slant steeper upward and in a
short time they were all quite tired. The floor of this little woods
was clean as the pine needles were so thick underfoot that no
grass or weeds had grown up. Max was thinking how nice it
would be to rest on this pine-straw mattress when Knipper
stopped and looked up into a tall tree. The others followed his
gaze.

Max was amazed when he saw the owl. It was much
larger than he had imagined. He had seen Saw-whet Owls
and Barn Owls before, but they were not much bigger than his
fist. Here, perched in solemn dignity, was a Long-Eared Owl.
It sat erect, twin tufts of feathers jutted from the head looking
like two curved horns. Its eyelids were closed to the day, but
it seemed somehow not to be sleeping; perhaps in deep
thought instead. Max realized the bird was nearly the size of
Fanzig and he had no idea how wide the folded wings might
stretch. He caught sight of powerful talons clamped around

the tree limb and had second thoughts about waking this old one.

"Fletcher! Old fellow! Hello! It's your friend, Knipper, the shepherd. Wake, old friend!"

The owl shuddered as if dreaming, then moved a little on his perch. One of his eyelids slid up. The bird blinked to look at the party calling to him from the ground. He was still silent and made only the tiniest movements of his head to view them.

At last the creature spoke. "Who . . . are *you*?" The voice was as calm as a blue sky and if the owl was surprised to see the strange collection of creatures below, he did not show it. "Oh yes . . . you are . . . Knipper." He was quiet again and Max began to wonder if he would say anything more. "It seems to be I have something to say to you, but it leaves me for the moment. No bother . . . it will come in good time. Who are these?" The bird bent forward on the limb. "I know Scrugnit well enough, even blindfolded and bound. But who are his captors and what do you seek of this old one?"

Max bowed; he felt the owl was indeed very old. "I am Max, good Fletcher. I am a prince of Gaspaar, son of King Randrew. This is Jippit Jumpjilter, an elf and great friend to me and a help to the shepherd Dimbarrel."

"In truth?" the owl replied. "It is a very long time since a son of King Todd has come to these mountains. This must be a good thing for one to see. I am glad to have seen it. Yes." The owl paused again before continuing. "I see you are an *elf-friend* and travel with two of the speaking ones. This is a wondrous thing. What *age* are you, Prince Max, that you have gained such companions and journeyed so far?"

Max blushed. "Old enough, sir. . . I am thirteen."

The owl seemed to laugh, or rather hooted in a laughing manner, but its eyes stayed locked on the prince when it spoke. "How *old* you are is a question you may not yet answer. I do not mean the years you have lived, but how far have one's thoughts grown."

Fanzig spoke. "It is good to meet the Fletcher of Runruggel, a legend among legends."

Fletcher turned his eyes slowly to the fox. "I have heard your name as well, good fox. I have forgotten it for the moment, but it will come in good time. What do you say of this Prince of Gaspaar?"

Fanzig sat down to answer. "He is the first to listen to the beasts in a long time. He wishes to learn."

Fletcher turned back to Max. "The fox speaks well of you, young Prince. Fletcher, too, has waited long to be heard by man. To help again. In what way am I to serve you?"

Max told the owl everything, leaving nothing out. He finished with the capture of Scrugnit and how they had learned of the witch's evil plan. ". . . So, I have now not even a treasure to hunt. My path seems to end," he said.

Fletcher was silent so long after Max finished his tale that the prince was afraid he had fallen to sleep with his eyes open. Then the owl said, "It occurs to me that I *do* know of such a treasure as you seek. A great treasure. But it is long ago and must come from deep in. It has been long since I have thought of it. Still . . . "

Jippit Jumpjilter had been quiet longer than he could stand. "Come on then! What is it? Where is it? Do you know or don't you?"

Max frowned at Jippit. "Don't worry him about it. I am the same way with my arithmetic. Father says better slow and sure, than fast and false."

The elf shook his head in disgust and began to pace back and forth. "Arithmetic!" he muttered under his breath, "What has *arithmetic* to do with adventure?"

Scrugnit chuckled. His old sneer had returned. "It seems when all is said and done, your road comes to an end here, young Prince. You will be in Her Wickedness' hand in a short while. Better to let me go now . . . she might not be so angry then."

Jippit boxed the dwarf's ears. "That should occupy your ears for the time being! Better to keep your mouth shut and mind your *own* troubles, Scrugnit. You are in our hands now and a witch that would set a dwarf against an elf doesn't sound too frightening to me."

Fletcher was taking no notice of the two quarreling below him. "Wait . . . yes . . . yes, of course." He blinked one round yellow eye and it seemed to Max he smiled. "I recall it now. The greatest treasure in the land. Yes. Quite."

"*Well?*" Jippit strained to keep from shouting.

All of them waited as Fletcher stroked a patch of ruffled feathers. Only Scrugnit was not concerned, he rubbed his throbbing ears against his shoulders to ease the pain. Fletcher looked up.

"The treasure is in the witch's tower where it has lain for years upon years."

They all gasped except for Knipper, who just nodded. "Of course, and tell them where the witch's tower stands," the dog sighed.

"At the top of Tarrand-Kitil —"

"The *Dragon's Back*," Knipper explained.

"At the top of Tarrand-Kitil," Fletcher continued, "beneath the broken crest, the foul Lake Doom lies gray with bubbling steam where once fire showered from deep in the earth. At the center of this dread pool, upon a large black rock, stands the tower of the witch. From there she has plotted and planned evils of which you may not guess. Many a knight has tried that tower. None have returned."

Max could hardly speak. His heart was pounding. "Is .
. . is she there, now?"

The owl opened a talon and stretched it. "Who can say?
She rides a creature of darkness, a nightmare to ride the night
wind. The dwarf would know the answer better than I. To see
the truth in his words would be as trying to see the bottom of
Lake Doom itself."

Max had begun to feel a mingled sense of excitement
and fear when Fletcher had spoken of the witch's tower. It was
as if everything in his life — everything that had ever
happened to him — was just so he would be here at just this
moment hearing of the witch's tower. He wanted to go away,
as far from the mountains as he could go. He tried to think
how he would feel back home at his father's palace. Instead,
all he could think of was the tower on dark Lake Doom. He
wished he knew what to do.

"Now this, *this* is a real elf adventure!" Jippit Jumpjilter
clapped his hands together and rubbed them in glee. "There's
a great tale in this, I'll wager."

Max tried not to sound nervous as he spoke. "You say
a — great treasure?"

Fletcher began to walk the branch which bent lower
with his weight. "The greatest treasure. It took years to steal
it, you can be sure, but she is too greedy to spend a coin of
it."

Max's mouth was dry. "How long would it take to reach
the tower?"

"I've never had to climb it myself," the owl chuckled. "I
should think the best of three days for a prince your size."

"That would take most of your time, wouldn't it, Max?
To the top and back again?" Knipper asked.

"Of course," Fanzig said, "it is a great and dangerous
adventure. All of us know your courage. None would blame

you should you choose not to go."

Max's throat was dry, and his legs felt unsteady as well now, because he knew that he would go. He heard himself speaking. "I don't suppose I have much choice if I still wish to finish this quest."

"Don't be a *fool*, boy!" Scrugnit sounded angry but a little afraid as well, Max thought.

"Better a fool than a coward!" Jippit boxed the dwarf's ears again. "At least he's not both, as are certain dwarves here about."

Fletcher closed his eyes. "I remember now my message for you, Knipper. Dimbarrel grows well. His nephew travels to the valley. He should be there within a few days. A rather talkative Jay came by yesterday with the news. Sad little fellow, really, doesn't know any other speaking birds. He just bubbles over when he sees me."

"Can you show us the way?" Max asked about the treasure.

"Of course," came the reply. "It will be easy to find. Evil always is. But the climb will be both cold and hard. You must make your mind up to it now or you will never see it through."

Jippit laughed. "We've seen more than a little trouble in the last few days. I should think a short climb would be simple enough exercise."

"I should save my mirth," Fletcher said as he flexed his other talon. "You may well need it later, good elf. I shall come to Dimbarrel's cabin tonight and explain the way to you. My eyes are open to the night for you. As for the day . . . I will continue my rest, if you don't mind."

Max bowed. "Good day, noble Fletcher."

The owl blinked in answer and then closed his great eyes. In an instant he became a statue again, hardly alive, it seemed.

The small party turned in silence and walked back out of the trees.

Max's eyes sought out the ragged peaks of the Runruggles ranged about them. Even on this clear summer day they looked dark and cold and now slightly evil. He shook his head and looked again. Forbidding they might be, dangerous perhaps, but they were still the grandest sight in all of the kingdom.

CHAPTER 23

THE BROTHERS NEAR THEIR FATES

They returned to the cabin as twilight drew near. After securing Scrugnit in the chicken coop they went about preparing supper. Since joining them, Jippit had become their chef and set them all to work at different tasks.

As Max sat chopping onions, he thought of something

that had been bothering him since he had learned of the witch's plan. She had sent him after a false treasure that would work evil, so what about Derek and Gerald? What terrible plans might she have set for his brothers? He hated to think of that. He did not worry so much for Derek. He had thought his oldest brother would be able to see through any scheme. This wasn't always true, but Max had believed it for a long time and he wanted to believe it now. But what of Gerald? He was the curious one, so eager to get to the secret of anything mysterious or magical. Max wondered what Gerald might have done had he been sent for the tree instead of him.

Thinking this, Max felt fear but also a sense of shame for doubting Gerald. If only he could be here with him sharing all the good things he was learning. He would see the plans of the witch for himself. But it had been long since he had truly talked with Gerald. The middle brother had not had much time for him in these last years. There were other things he was more interested in. Max felt bitterness at this memory but there was the cold uneasy feeling again. He had been more upset at feeling ignored than really caring about the change in his brother. The tears on Max's cheek were not just from the onions he was chopping. He prayed that Gerald would be safe, and Derek as well, and vowed he would be a better brother if they all got home. He felt better after this, and had little trouble eating a hearty supper.

The moon was clear in the early night sky when Max heard a soft flapping. With a sudden whoosh, Fletcher, the great long eared owl, lit upon the windowsill. The bird made a short hop to the table and folded his wings as he eyed the others.

Jippit Jumpjilter jumped to his feet. "*Late* enough you arrive, Old One! Now, tell us the way to the scagg's tower."

Fletcher turned his head to Max. "Are you as ready to assault Tarrand-Kitil as your companion, young master?"

Max rubbed his neck as he answered. "I am not so eager to rush on as Jippit, but I am ready."

"A good answer," the owl replied. "Now I shall show you the way you must follow." Fletcher bent to overturn a small salt bowl with his beak. With a single claw-tip he carefully traced their path in the spilled grains. When he was certain they understood the way, he straightened up. "You will need heavy clothing as you reach the top of the mountain," he said. "There is even unnatural ice on the cliffs above the lake." Then he added, "There is one thing more you must know, young Max. The witch has placed a strong spell upon her tower. Should anyone, or anything, leave the tower against her wish, the tower, and even the little island, will sink into the depths of Lake Doom. You must be mindful of this once you have gained the treasure."

After much discussion they decided that Knipper and Fanzig would stay behind at the farm as well as Blueberry. Knipper must watch the sheep and Fanzig had to agree that the more of them that traveled, the longer it would take to make the climb. And of course, Blueberry would be no help climbing the steep mountain.

"It is you and I then, Jumpjilter," Max said.

"And Scrugnit," the elf replied.

Fletcher nodded. "Yes, you will need the dwarf. He alone knows where the boat is hidden by which you must cross Lake Doom. I suppose he might know of any dangers of the tower as well."

"He will not want to tell us," Max answered.

"Oh, he will be glad enough to tell us," Jippit grinned. "You just must ask him in the right manner."

Max looked at the owl and sighed. "It will not be easy."

Then he quickly added, "Please, Knipper, don't say it! I know, 'no true adventure is easy.'"

The dog laughed and they all felt relief in the laughter.

"I will watch for the witch," Fletcher said. "I will come to your aid if you should need it. I am hopeful that you won't."

After that they all said goodnight and went to their different beds to rest. Everyone except Fletcher, that is. He nibbled at a few scraps on the table, dropped them and shook his head. Pausing on the window ledge he studied the night wind and then turned back to the empty room. "The heart of Gaspaar beats true in this house tonight," he said quietly. "May it be strong for the days before it." And then he was gone.

In the morning Jippit and Max assembled clothes for the cold heights. Dimbarrels's heavy wool winter coats were hooded and came almost to Max's feet. The arms were so long neither of them could poke a hand out of them. "I have money in my bag to buy Dimbarrel new coats," Max said as they cut the arms to the proper length. Still, Max was almost swallowed in the shepherd's garb. The gloves that Knipper brought them were very awkward. Fanzig could not help laughing at the sight of the boy and the elf wrapped up with the collars up to their noses.

Jippit replied dryly, "Laugh if you must, we look no more foolish than knights do in their bulky armor!"

Max disagreed but did not argue.

Fanzig had an idea that they could fit the coat sleeves, they had cut off, over their britches. "It will keep your legs warmer near the top of Tarrand-Kitil."

They had a difficult time getting enough left-over wool to fit Scrugnit. Jippit said the cold would be good for the dwarf, but Max made sure he would be clothed as warmly as they were and packed coats for all.

"I'll not forget your kindness, Master Max," the dwarf said.

Max worried more when the dwarf acted kind than when he sounded angry. He could tell it made Jippit uneasy too.

Having packed everything they would need, the small band set off. They would change into their mountain clothes when they had mounted the rocky side of Tarrand-Kitil.

At the edge of the valley, Fanzig and Knipper said goodbye.

Max was sad to leave the two friends behind. "Take good care of Blueberry until I return," he said.

"She awaits your return as we do," Knipper replied. "Courage, Prince Max!" The dog turned to Jippit. "Sir Jumpjilter, this is as fine an adventure as any elf might hope for. Be worthy of it!"

Jippit said nothing but turned away to follow the route Fletcher had shared with them. Max looked up at the mountain they were marching toward and thought, *"And now to the treasure – or the witch."*

***

Derek

The young Earl of Kurn kicked the burnt wooden embers of the barn out of the way. Powdery ash billowed in a cloud that sent him coughing. "Curse that infernal dragon!" he swore. "I would give all my land and last gold to see his grinning beak stuck on the gate at the king's palace!"

Derek waited for the earl to settle down again. All their conversations since Derek had reached the empty village had ended with him losing his temper.

"Your Lordship," Derek replied, "your anger will do little good if you spend it kicking and spitting at the remains of your town. Sir Claire, to whom I was a squire, once told me that anger only helps your enemy win control of you. A plan of battle is better than a dozen rash swords."

The earl laughed harshly. "Don't get mad — get even, say you?"

"Something as like. Though I should say getting even with a beast, is a useless thought."

The earl pointed a soot-covered finger at Derek. "But dragons are not beasts. Beasts do not make bargains. My serfs tell me this one made a bargain years ago and other villages have dealt with the fiend all along the coast."

Derek shook his head. "Well, it is certain I must needs be careful. This creature is no simple wolf or bear with merely a big appetite."

"Appetite? Not for food! It burned more up than it ate by a hundred. Truly, I do not think I saw it eat a thing. Foul magic is working here, Sir Knight! I did not believe it either, until it came last week, and did all you see. Now I pledge you all I have if you will find this fiend and kill it for me."

Derek frowned. "Nay, Sire. I shall not take a coin to do a deed of chivalry. Should I succeed, I'll take my claim from its dead clutches."

"Spoken fair!" the earl shouted. "Praise the day! You shall have a solid meal and your horse groomed well for such a fight as you intend. We are still eating the charred remains of my herds. Hard meat, salted deep, is not tasty fare, but it will remind you to avoid the fiery breath of the dragon."

"Do you have knowledge of where this great worm's lair is hidden, my lord?"

The earl snorted. "Hardly. Though the old man said that every full moon he carried gold or silver at father's request to a wide flat rock in the middle of Forest Quist. It is somewhere between those two peaks yonder. Before the dragon came, I had scoffed that no one farmed that valley. It is little wonder it has grown so wild. They say it is always night in there, and the full moon approaches within three days."

"Then I shall ride for the flat rock and see what may be seen." Saying this, the prince took provisions from the servants and climbed again upon Moonstone's saddle.

"Grace guide your hand, Sir Knight!" the Earl of Kurn called. "Who shall I say rides forth to meet Gorackle?"

Derek grinned. "Say it was Derek, a son of King Randrew, a rider for Gaspaar."

"So shall it be in song and story!" the earl shouted after him as Derek rode from the burned fields and into the great forest of Quist.

***

Gerald

Gerald gazed into the flickering flame at the center of the chamber. When he closed his eyes now, he could see it just as clearly. A green glow rippled behind his eyelids. He had watched his teacher, the wizard Gorna, draw patterns in the cool powdery dust on the floor and chant incantations in some language Gerald did not know. Even so, the words seemed to hold a grip on his mind, making shapes in the darkness that filled in like images in a dream. Sweet incense burning in censers made everything hazy in his mind. The Duchess explained that all these things were merely ways to pull off the illusions and lies that men accepted in every waking day. Here, in the dark, she said, the inner eye must be opened, and the great hidden power might be approached.

Gorna stepped nearer the fire and held up his hand to

177

the apprentices sitting in the circle. "I have received a summons to the north. I shall return within two or three days at most. Spend the time in practice of the shapes and forms. I will examine you when I return. The Council shall see who is worthy of the next gate."

Gerald smiled. He saw the Council's game. They intended to bring him under their control, to make servants of these pupils. It was obvious, but they were mistaken about him. He was a prince already and knew the way of power. He would take all they gave him and, with his own mind, rise above these prideful ones. Despite their haughty words he sensed their fear of each other, as well as the mysterious power they approached. He would be king and master when all was done, he promised himself.

Yet with these thoughts was another consideration that never left Gerald's mind. The Duchess. Yes, she alone was a peer to him. She saw through these muttering old fools as well. Perhaps she truly did seek a worthy king to share her throne. He did not fear her, but was a little in awe of her, for her beauty was mystery. Mystery pleased Gerald more than all else. He wished she should soon return so she might see how far he stood above these others.

***

Max

The day was hot, and Max wondered how they could ever need the heavy wool coats they carried in their packs. Scrugnit said nothing as they traveled, and Max was grateful.

As evening began to settle, he studied the rough outline of the peak before them. The top seemed broken and jagged, and he knew beneath those ragged cliffs, Lake Doom reflected the rising moon in its cold gray waters.

The night passed quickly. Max had slept hard after all their marching. He knew Jippit had tied Scrugnit too well to escape and had not worried. They ate only cold food now. They would light no fires this close to Tarrand-Kitil. They dared not guess if eyes atop the dark tower searched for just such a sign.

The second day was harder hiking. The ground sloped more and more upwards and grew quickly steeper. Max was soon tiring but hated to say so in front of Scrugnit. He would fall behind and then run hard to catch up, only to fall back again after a bit more of the march. He was amazed at the strength of his two companions. The dwarf certainly looked strong enough, even bulky, but not the elf.

Jippit Jumpjilter was the most incredible man Max had ever met. Of course, he was also the only elf he had met. There was just no telling what he would say or do next. Though he was a serious fellow, often not speaking for long stretches, Max had misjudged him at their first meeting. He knew he was fortunate to have such a friend.

"Well, now," Jippit said, stopping, "let's have a bite of lunch. Here, beneath this oak. It's likely the last we will see for a time."

They sat down in the shade of the tree. Max was very thankful the elf got hungry, even if he did not get tired. As they finished their meal he asked, "What do you mean this shall be one of the last trees we shall see?" He hoped the elf would talk a while longer before starting the march again.

"Not last tree . . . last oak. The higher . . . the drier. Old man oak likes a good drink. From here on it will be pine and aspen." The elf looked up at the peak of Tarrand-Kitil, just visible through the low hanging clouds. "Up there no trees are happy. Just rock and ice."

The more they hiked, the darker the sky grew. Clouds

were gathering about the mountains and the color of the forest began to dim. It was as if life itself were pulling back from the rocky giant they neared.

It was more climb than march now and fewer of even the pines and aspens marked their way. Max saw that Tarrand-Kitil was barer than any of her neighbors. "*A poison place,*" he heard Knipper saying, "*you shall hear no bird calls and see no tracks there.*" This was grim enough and now the wind was rising. Though this cooled their hot march, Max did not like the low moaning as it blew over the rocky ground.

The twilight sky was giving way to darkness when they came out of the sparse forest. They stood upon the edge of a small clearing which ran straight into the actual wall of the mountain. The bulk of rock jutted steeply up and up so they had to look straight overhead to see the last daylight slipping behind the giant shadow. Max could see the outline of the broken peaks of Tarrand-Kitil. They did indeed appear like the spiny back of a dragon.

It was pitch dark as they laid their blankets on the pine needles at the edge of the wood. Max was almost asleep when the thunder began to rumble round the mountain. Far away clumping turned to shattering bellows as lightning lit the bare rock walls of Tarrand-Kitil. The wind blew harder and harder. Max grabbed the dry needles tightly in his hands as the mountain seemed to wake like some creature of the night. The winds called out to him with taunting moans, daring him to come closer. He shut his eyes but could see clearly in his mind the peak where waited the tower of the witch. He had been running from danger since he left the inn, Max thought. Now he was rushing toward it. Each step took him closer. He was even climbing after it. Was this not even more foolish than to search for the magic tree? What wisdom was this? Did he dare to think himself a bold knight to tempt such powers? His skin prickled as the questions burned in his mind. With horror he pictured the face of the "Duchess" and he heard her laughter in the thunder peeling down the slopes, pouring into the trees, searching him out.

***

The Duchess

The lady in deep purple stepped from the door of her tower and looked out on the dark storm clouds that boiled beyond the rocky landing. Lightning crashed nearby and the crack of thunder blew her cape wide. Ignoring the fierce weather, she turned to look back up at the slender stone fortress behind her and at the one light that burned in the highest window. "Keep well, young one," she said with a cruel grin, "I've other matters to attend." She brought a small silver whistle to her lips and blew. In a few moments there was a shrill cry over the wind and a shadow flickered in the lightning as it neared the mist-shrouded tower. A creature with the form of a horse yet winged and covered in dark silk skirting alighted before her. The beast's breath curled in wispy trails from its wide nostrils, and its eyes glowed yellow. She moved to the side of the dark shape and raised herself up onto the saddle, wrapping her legs together on the near side. "To the borders of Empt, cold one!" she commanded. As the leathery wings unfolded and beat the air, the lady considered her plans. They were all working their way like the tendrils of a weed slowly choking the life from a neglected garden.

181

CHAPTER 24

THE CLIMB BEGINS

The morning sky was a light gray overhead, and the only sound was the lazy rustling of the pines in the early breeze. Max had never been so happy to see daylight. Sitting up, he stretched and noticed the visitor.

Perched on a short branch not far above Max, Fletcher sat in slumber. The great eyes were closed and only the tufts of his tall ears moved softly in the morning air. Max was happy to see him there and wondered how long the owl had watched over them in the night. It was a comforting thought. "Good morning, Old Fletcher," he called.

The owl drew its head down closer to its folded wings and stretched a long brown wingtip out as if to mark some point in the wood. An eyelid rose and Fletcher settled back to his earlier stance. He addressed his host in his usual formal manner. "Good morning to you also, young Prince . . . I trust you slept well?"

"Very little, I'm afraid. The storm was so loud it kept me awake." Max was embarrassed to admit his fear.

Fletcher blinked. "I would not be too bothered with thunder and lightning at the present. There are, however, a few other problems to be faced I should perhaps feel concerned by."

Max rubbed his eyes. "I . . . I thought I heard 'Her' last night."

The owl considered this. "Yes . . . she was in her tower. I had come to tell you. Still, it seems a wonder you would hear her."

"So, the witch is home, is she?" Jippit Jumpjilter was rolling up his blanket. "Well, that is her great misfortune."

"I . . . probably was dreaming," Max said blushing.

"But then she is a great laugher," the owl continued. "I've heard her cackle . . ."

"Cackle, brackle, jackal!" Jippit broke in. "Has she seen us?"

"Seen you? Oh no, no, I would not think so," Fletcher said coming back to his news. "She isn't there now at all. She has ridden her dark mount far from here long before the sunrise. That is what I have come to tell you."

"How may a horse travel in such country?" Max wanted to know. "I left Blueberry behind thinking she could not make the climb."

"Her mare is of the night wind, young Max," Fletcher's

eyes were cold. "It is a spell, a phantom. She may fly but at night and must seek shadow in the day's light."

"She is real enough when the moon grins down all cold and bloodthirsty!" Scrugnit leered.

Fletcher went on as if he had not heard the dwarf. "I shall continue to watch for the witch and keep you aware of her movements. The word is that she has been here and there, moving over a wide span of country, even as far north as Empt itself. No doubt she keeps many cauldrons boiling. Much movement in a witch is a bad sign. You must make haste. Time is no certain ally." The owl bid them a farewell and left in a long silent glide under the shadows of the pines.

"Good enough. Let's not dilly dally here longer." Jippit stretched his arms over his head and turned to face the dwarf who lay bound under a nearby tree. "We'll have no more of your lolly-gagging today, Scrugnit. Drag your feet and you'll get a tighter leash. We must untie your hands for this climbing now but be warned. We'll all be tied together and I'm a master of elf knots. Just pick at your rope once to admire my skill and I'll whittle your thumbs off! Then you can dig at the tying as much as you wish."

Scrugnit made a face at the elf but said nothing.

After they had packed up again, Jippit tied them in a line with Scrugnit to lead, followed by Jippit, and Max at the rear. They were each tied about ten feet apart.

"In the hard places we should keep near the end of our rope," Jippit said. "If one of us should stumble, the rope won't jerk the others loose from the rocks as well."

After this they walked across the little field to the very side of the towering height. Jippit stopped and pulled a bright green ring from his left hand, kissed it and set it in a narrow crack in the rock. Looking up at the mountain, he spoke solemnly.

"I'll claim you again when this adventure's done, Ring of Jasper Jumpjilter. If I should not return, I shall bid your master greetings."

Max looked away as Jippit made this elfin oath but wondered why Scrugnit had kept silent. Perhaps the dwarf honored such things, he thought, or else he was afraid that Jippit would pay him harshly for any remark he might make.

They began the ascent.

The climb was not so hard as Max had imagined it would be — at first. They found their way easily enough, but soon the rocks became more jagged. Max saw there were almost no plants now, no trees, just a scraggly bush sprouting from the rock here and there. Far rockier than its neighbors, Tarrand Katil seemed even colder to the touch than he would expect, as if it were an unnatural place.

The clouds kept the sun from beating down as much as it had on their march from the farm. Still, Max did not like the look of the dark sky as it grumbled and threatened overhead. They had to stop and rest several times and he knew it was because he kept falling back. Jippit never said anything but was always ready to go again after just a few minutes. The young prince hated to be the one to slow them down.

Max could tell his boots were not made for mountain climbing and hoped they would last the journey. His legs and arms were becoming a mass of bruises, but he tried not to complain. Once he bumped his shin so hard, he wanted to scream but bit his lip to keep quiet. A silent tear worked down his dusty face, but he had not made a sound. He wondered if Derek had ever climbed a mountain such as this.

Tired as he was, Max was awed to watch the elf and dwarf as they scaled the rocks. Scrugnit looked sturdy enough, but Jippit seemed light as a feather and almost bounced from boulder to boulder. There must be mountains in Elfenland, he thought.

The most miserable thing was whenever Jippit had to help pull Max over a bit of steep rock face or push him up onto a difficult ledge. This happened too often for comfort and more often as the day grew older.

They were taking a rest on a rounded ledge when Scrugnit shouted. "Storm! Quick, to the cave!"

Max and Jippit turned to see a great thunderhead rolling toward them over the valley below. It seemed as large as the mountain itself and bright forks of lightning flashed in its dark swirls. It would be upon them in moments. Looking out over the valley, Max saw for the first time just how high they had climbed. His breath seemed short, and he was — in a moment — dizzy. Everything started to swim before his eyes. Max sat and grabbed hold of a large boulder to gain back his balance. Flattening himself against the mountain, he closed his eyes and tried not to think of the long drop below.

"Come on, Max! Come on! This is no time to rest!" Jippit called. "Scrugnit knows a cave near here!" Then, seeing Max pressed against the rock, Jippit guessed what was wrong. "Crawl after me!" he called. "Don't look at anything but the rocks!"

Scrugnit moved quickly now. He knew where the cave was and hurried to reach it, impatient with the pair joined to him by the elf's rope. "Hurry! Hurry! We will all be swept off the mountain like flies if you tarry longer!"

Max got his breath back but did not dare to look up from the rock as he crawled after Jippit's taut line. The line provided an arrow of direction just below his face and was his only comfort as he fought to concentrate on following the elf. The wind moaned louder, and a chill washed over them as the thunderhead pushed in. Then they were at the dwarf's promised cave. Max tumbled into the cool darkness, grateful to be away from the ledge and out of the storm.

They had just entered the slender fissure in the rocks when the storm crashed into the mountain. Thunder echoed through the cave and lightning lit the darkness around them in bright flashes as they huddled against the cold walls.

Max held his ears against the booming thunder. The rain was driving so hard he imagined a legion of goblins hammering at the mountain with their fists. Through the opening he could see the rain bouncing as it hit. Then he saw that it wasn't rain at all. The hail was the size of large marbles and Max was thankful to be inside the little cavern.

Night was falling now, and Max pulled his great coat out to use as an extra blanket. When the lightning flashed, he saw that the dwarf was watching him with a crafty smile. Max turned away. He was glad that Jippit could see in the dark. The storm was too loud for talk, so he decided to stay awake until he and Jippit could talk about their plans for the next day. But the prince fell asleep listening to the hail.

CHAPTER 25

TREACHERY

He was awake and something was wrong. It was so quiet Max could hear water dripping off the rocks outside the cave. He remembered he had felt the same way in the tunnel under the mountains. He could tell it was early morning. Out of the corner of his eye, he saw something move. A shadow fell over him and he closed his eyes, knowing he was being watched. After a moment he carefully peeked and saw Scrugnit creeping to stand over the sleeping Jumpjilter. The dwarf bent in silence to slip the elf's dagger from its sheath without a tug. Max wondered desperately what he might do. To call to Jippit would be useless. Scrugnit would stab him before he could stir. He was tensing to jump at the dwarf when he saw the rope.

Scrugnit was still tied to Jippit and the slack line ran right beside Max. Just as the dwarf drew back for the killing blow, Max grabbed the rope and jerked with all his might.

Scrugnit had raised the knife high over his head when the rope pulled tight. He spun, surprised and angry, tumbling backwards with a shout. Before Max could draw his own sword, Jippit and Scrugnit were wrestling all over the rough floor of the cave. Each of them held tightly to the dagger, grunting and hollering as they fought to wrench it free of the other's grasp.

Gripping his sword, Max rushed at the two struggling men. Just as he came on them, a kick from the dwarf sent him reeling back across the cave. Before he could catch his breath, he saw Scrugnit bite the elf's shoulder so hard he yelled and let go of the dagger.

Now they were standing, and the dwarf was backing Jippit out of the cave and onto the narrow ledge. Scrugnit was laughing as he stalked the elf.

Max's stomach went into a knot as he remembered yesterday's sudden fear. Outside on the ledge the mountain dropped away to nothing — but his friend was in danger. He clutched his sword again and hurried toward the opening shutting his mind to the long fall below.

Emerging from the cave, Max found Jippit was balancing on a rock which jutted out from the mountain wall. The elf waited in a wrestler's crouch for the laughing dwarf approaching him with the dagger. Max took a short glance over the edge and rushed on. He gave a loud cry and swung the flat side of the blade as hard as he could at the dwarf's legs. The iron smacked loud against Scrugnit's right knee, bowling him over the ledge. The dwarf screamed in terror as he went over the side of the mountain. At just that moment Max saw they were all still tied together and Jippit was already being plucked off the rock. He hardly had a chance to yell as he too was jerked after the elf and the dwarf.

Much to Max's surprise and relief, the fall ended almost as soon as it began. They fell directly onto another ledge just some eight feet below their own. The dwarf shouted in pain as the elf and then the boy fell on top of him.

Jippit had the dagger now as they sat on the ledge rubbing their bruises. Scrugnit moaned wearily, but there were no broken bones among them. Max and Jippit laughed and laughed for quite a while. It was the first time Max had ever seen tears in Jippit's eyes.

It was much colder here than Max had realized the day before and they finally pulled on the great wool coats. He thought they looked like poorly stuffed bear dolls in the brown woolen wraps.

Tarrand Katil was unlike any of its sister heights and Max did not doubt the magical legends of its creation. The climbing grew much steeper now and often Scrugnit would be just over Jippit's head with Max directly beneath them both. Max had not been frightened of the height since the morning's excitement but did not look down any more often than he had to.

When they stopped for the night again Max studied his gloves. The sharp rocks were wearing them away. His arms ached, his back ached, but nothing ached so badly as his poor, tired legs. He ached so much he forgot to be afraid of what lay ahead. Climbing was so difficult he could really not think much of anything else.

Jippit had tied Scrugnit's hands again and turned to Max as he sat down to rest. "Tomorrow we reach Lake Doom," he said.

Max nodded. He was too tired to talk. He slept soundly without even a worried thought of the witch's tower.

"No . . . not yet." Max was not ready to wake. Jippit Jumpjilter kept on shaking him. "No, Jippit, just another few minutes! The mountain will still be here tomorrow."

Jumpjilter scoffed in his old manner. "Of course. The mountain will be here tomorrow, as you say. Then, so might the witch!"

You could never out talk this fellow, Max thought. "Then give me some cheese and bread," he said, sitting up. "I must have an empty head to have come here, but my stomach will not be."

Jippit laughed and slapped him on the shoulder. "You are not the soft butter you were when we met at the Willtil, young Max. You're not a solid cheese yet, but I have not seen many firmer jams."

"You'll both be jam for her wickedness soon enough," Scrugnit sneered. "She'll have you spread on toast, my fine Prince."

The last climb was the hardest. Sometimes the rock was so steep that even Jippit had to fall back and try some other way. He swore at Scrugnit each time this happened. The dwarf would just shrug and say he'd forgotten which way that particular ridge ran or how steep that face was.

Max knew the dwarf would give them as much trouble as he could now. He wondered how they would ever get him to show them the boat if they did get to Lake Doom. But as set to slow them as Scrugnit seemed to be, Jippit Jumpjilter was twice as determined to make the top.

Max scrambled on as well as he could. He was happy to find the soreness left him as he struggled up the rock. It was not so hard as he learned to climb. Watching Jippit was the best training he would find anywhere this side of Elfenland, he decided. Max tried to do everything as he saw Jippit do it. Soon he began to feel he was no longer fighting against the mountain but seeking the way it opened for him. The stairs were rough, but in elf fashion he was learning to see them.

***

Derek

The trees of the forest of Quist were tall and thick. Daylight was choked down long before it reached the forest floor. Derek walked Moonstone beneath the dark tent, weaving past the trunks that rose high above. Without a guide he had only the knowledge that the flat stone of the dragon's bargain was somewhere near the middle of this great wood. He had spent the best part of three days tracking through twisting thickets. The brambles liked the dark and the wild vines crawled the trunks and snaked between the branches to reach the distant light. Derek talked to his horse as he guided him along the way.

"This forest is too quiet, Moonstone. Every sound here echoes. All sounds seem too far away. If I were the type to imagine evil sights, I'd imagine them here. Well, tonight is another full moon by the earl's account. Still, no sense worrying now, as Sir Claire used to tell me. 'Plenty of time to be scared later, my lad. And if we die, then we've wasted no time being afraid.' And Sir Quinn was a good one for advice, as well. 'You know a little trick I do, boy? When I feel fear come creeping up, I grin. Big…like this.'" Derek started to laugh as he felt the muscles of his cheeks go tight. His laugh stopped in his throat at the sight of what stood in his path ahead.

It was a white stag. A tall, proud, deer with a rack of antlers greater than any Derek had ever seen. His heart shivered at the sheer beauty of the creature. It eyed him steadily, as if marking him as friend or foe.

Derek whispered to Moonstone, "By all the stories, that is the finest free creature I've ever seen. It is like the very one told in the quests of King Arthur. If we were on no other course, Moonstone, I should turn after that creature and ride with all my will. I feel it has a noble heart and the hunter in me would risk all for the chase. Indeed, does it not seem to challenge us now to follow? Yet, who knows what such a race might bring? Still, can a sign as strong as this be ignored, when no other marks our way?" He gripped the reins of the charger slowly and raised his heels. "Not by me!" he shouted, "Ha! Away!" He kicked his heels in, launching Moonstone to speed. Derek whipped the reins as the great horse burst ahead with an energy it had held in check for many days.

The stag sprung also, at the same moment, and now the chase was on. The great deer bounced and bounded over root and thicket. It twisted and turned with its white tail raised behind, like a flag beckoning the hunters to follow. Derek was amazed that Moonstone, though large for the unmarked trail, could match speed against the wild thing of the wood. They rushed ahead, loud hoof-beats and broken branches, snapping and cracking as they ran their determined course, with only the sight of the darting animal to guide them. As the minutes passed in dizzying flight, the prince felt his joy return as he urged Moonstone on. All fear of dragons was lost in this high chase through Forest Quist as the full moon grew brighter in the evening sky.

Max

Once again, the sky was darkening when Jippit signaled them to stop. He called softly to Max, "We are there."

Max had hardly looked above them until that moment. It had seemed that the mountain went on forever and he had given up trying to guess how far they were from the top. Now he saw that they were just beneath an overhang of gray rock and beyond that he could make out the tips of the icy cliffs, the "Dragon's Back" — Tarrand-Kitil.

The wind was picking up and trying to slip inside his clothes, but Max would have felt cold enough without it. He hardly dared to think of what lay above the overhang.

"You first, Max," Jippit said. "I must keep near Scrugnit and we must both hoist you up."

Max tried to show no fear as the two small men lifted him to their shoulders and pushed him up the rock. He put his gloved hands on the rim of the overhang and pulled. He half-crawled, half-flopped, over the edge before he looked up.

CHAPTER 26

LAKE DOOM

The first stars were pricking the sky as Max studied the top of Tarrand-Kitil. The jagged peaks that gave the mountain its name were black shadows with just a glint of ice on their tips. Below them, in a sunken rocky bowl, Lake Doom lay cold and gray with heavy steaming mists gliding across its surface. The lake was not as large as he had imagined, but he could not see the other side for the swirling vapors. For a moment Max could see nothing else, but then his eyes caught the outline of a dark cone sticking out of the clouds of steam. It made him think of a giant dunce cap, but he knew it could only be the tip of the witch's tower.

"Hello! Max!" Jippit called up from below the ledge. "Are you all right?"

Max took a last look at the darkened tower poking through the mists and crawled back to the ledge. "It's here," he called down.

"Well, we knew that, didn't we?" Jippit shot back. "Not much point in climbing up if we were just guessing!"

Max shook his head. He was too nervous to laugh, but he was glad that Jumpjilter seemed unworried.

When they had all gotten up, Scrugnit grinned. "Just go on right ahead, my boy. Her wickedness is expecting you, I'm sure."

Jippit frowned. "If she were back, I think old Fletcher would have let us know. I'm afraid we won't be able to count on her welcome, Scrugnit."

They moved carefully down the gently sloping wall to the lake. Max began to wonder if they could find the dwarf's ferry, if Scrugnit chose to keep silent.

"I suppose you are wondering just where I have tied my punt?" the dwarf snickered. "How I wish I could remember! What a shame for us all to come so far only to turn back here."

"Let us have a talk, good Max," Jippit said and walked some little distance from them after setting down his pack.

Max was certain that Jippit would want to argue about forcing the dwarf to speak of the boat. Though he could not agree to it, he almost wished to let the elf go ahead. But Jippit did not speak of that.

"Max, pretend to talk with me in low tones. In just a few moments our guide back there will see that I have forgotten my dagger is in my pack and will cut his rope. Then we shall simply follow him to his craft."

Max was open-mouthed with wonder at the elf's plan. "Jippit!" he whispered. "That's a great idea! Of course, he'll lead us right to it."

"You had better give me your sword. When we catch him again, I think he might respect the blade in my hand a bit more — not realizing your great ability, of course." The elf was smiling. "Don't look now," he said as he bent closer to Max, "but our good friend has nearly sawed through his line. We must be sure not to lose sight of him. But we must not catch him too soon, either. There, he is off now!"

Max turned to see the dwarf jumping over a rock and running silently toward the shadows of some large boulders on the lake's edge. He was moving so quickly it seemed he would vanish before they could follow. Max was about to warn of this when Jippit, dropping his own line, rushed past Max with his sword. The prince followed as fast as he could, but soon both the dwarf and the elf had vanished in the mist around the lake.

With the sky growing darker now the fog of Lake Doom was rolling up its banks. Max listened as hard as he could for any sound of the elf or dwarf. There was no hint of either, only the wind whispering through the rocks. He began following the bank of the lake in the direction Jippit had taken, walking slowly and studying each shadow carefully. He missed the sword and wondered what he would do if he met the dwarf first. It was growing much colder now as the night began and only the moon and stars lit the mountain top. Max decided to huddle down against a large boulder to shield himself from the wind and dug his hands inside his coat to warm them.

He was leaning back against the boulder when he noticed something odd. Two small puffs of frosty steam drifted from the other side of his shelter. That moment he noticed another puff just like them from his own mouth. It was his breath, frozen in the peak's cold night air.

Lying down, Max began to crawl around the back of the boulder. Peering into the dark shadow, he could just make out the outline of the dwarf pulling something by a rope. It was the dwarf's boat. In a moment Scrugnit would have it in the water and all their plans would be ruined.

Max would have charged his enemy, but Jippit had his sword. Still, there had to be a way, if only he could think of it. Lying there in the dark, Max suddenly remembered a game of hide-and-seek he had played long before, and a smile came to his face. Derek had used a clever trick to catch him then. He knew it had to work, must work, now. Grabbing a small stone near him, Max tossed it as hard as he could over the boulders to his left. He almost cheered when Scrugnit jumped around at the noise of the falling stone. He watched in anxious silence as the dwarf drew the dagger from his belt and slipped away to see what had made the sound. As soon as Scrugnit was gone, he hurried to the boat and shoved it into the slimy water. It was a very small craft, just a single-dwarf punt, but as he slid it across the pebbles, it scraped loudly against a stone and he knew Scrugnit had heard it.

Hearing Scrugnit's rushing footsteps, Max leaped into the boat and shoved away from the rocks. He was moving slowly into the edge of the fog when Scrugnit got to the water.

"Come back! Come back, lad!" The dwarf was shaking in anger. "You don't know Doom! You dare to dream of approaching the tower without Scrugnit? Watch the bubbles! Listen for the splashes, boy!" The dwarf was pacing the shore not ten feet from where Max sat in the punt, but he did not touch even a toe into the wet slime of Doom.

Max grabbed the short paddle of the craft and poked it into the lake to test the bottom. He dipped all but his hand into the water but felt nothing. Swallowing the lump that came to his throat, he tried to stay calm. When he looked up, he saw Jippit holding his sword to Scrugnit's chest.

"I wish you to drop the dagger, good dwarf. I would not care to dull this fine blade on your flinty heart." Jippit took the dagger from the scowling Scrugnit and called to Max. "You are safe, Max?"

Max beamed with relief. "Yes, Jippit Jumpjilter, I am quite safe. But beware the water's edge. The bottom must drop away here to who knows where." Paddling back to the rocky shore he realized with sudden dread that there was a problem that he had not foreseen. There was no other way. He took a deep breath. "Jippit . . . I must go on alone," he said.

The elf finished tying Scrugnit's hands and turned to the boy, then seeing his gaze looked down at the boat. "It's a very tight fit, I see, but I believe I can pack on board with you."

Max shook his head. "We might manage the two of us, but then there would be no room for a great treasure . . . it would sink us like a stone!"

Jippit stood silent for a long moment with his hands on his hips. He nodded. "So, it must be. Your treasure waits, good Prince. Let not your wits fail you. Bold adventure, for the crown of Gaspaar!" With that he drew his sword and solemnly held it out for Max to grasp.

Scrugnit gave a bitter shout. "A sword won't be much good in the great tower, boy! None have climbed those stairs without Her Wickedness' leave. Your nightmares crouch in the shadows, hungry for you! Go now to your *doom*!" The dwarf yelped as Jippit twisted his nose and boxed his ears.

Max wanted to say something to Jippit but could think of no words. He waved and began to paddle slowly into the mists.

CHAPTER 27

THE WITCH'S TOWER

The flat front of the boat disappeared in the white fog ahead of him as Max paddled toward the center of the lake. Sliding into the clouds of vapor he looked back to the shore. Already Jippit had vanished in the gray curtain.

Now he was alone, he thought, more alone than ever in his life. There was no one to even be afraid with. He turned his thoughts to the witch's tower and wondered how he would find it in the white blindness of the fog. As time passed, he began to wonder how he would find his way back to the shore.

It seemed he had been paddling for a long time now that he thought of it. *Am I going in circles?* The thought struck Max like a chilling blow. How would he ever escape? He stopped paddling and listened. He could hear the murmur of bubbles popping on the oily surface, but what was that splash? A fish? A fish at the top of Tarrand-Kitil? His mind raced, he tried not to think of what it might be, but perhaps this was Scrugnit's plan. Perhaps he had tricked him to take the boat so that some horrible water creature would catch him. Now Max was hearing many sounds in the fog; slaps and gurgles, splashes and plunks. "*A poison place*," he remembered Knipper's words. The dog didn't know the half of it, he decided. If only he could get back, he would have plenty to tell Knipper.

He began to paddle very fast and the sound of his paddle churning the water was a good sound to him. He was sure he must come out of the fog any moment now. Then, looking up, he gasped and threw himself down in the bottom of the punt.

***

Derek

The chase had lead Derek deep into the wildest part of the forest. Twice he had despaired of ever overtaking the stag, yet Moonstone always seemed ready to follow the invisible path. In each case, he would soon catch a glimpse of the proud antlered head poised in bright moonlight, almost as if waiting for them. The chase would start again, and Moonstone would surge forward. Though he might never catch the wondrous beast, the thrill of the chase was like a great draft of delicious wine to Derek. The sheer joy he felt was something he could hardly explain to others. Indeed, from that day he always compared delight in anything good with that feeling he had had when chasing the great stag.

Bursting through a heavy thicket, Derek found he had ridden onto open ground. The moon and stars shone brightly and in the wide clearing before them he saw a flat, table of stone. It was large enough for a pair of wagons to rest on, raised by four stone pillars as high as a man's chest. The shock of discovering the table was no greater than the sight of the stag running before him, leaping high atop the stone, skidding to a halt. The animal turned to face his pursuer. Moonstone rushed on, breathing hard, sweat coursing down the horse's bruised sides.

Something shifted against Derek's chest and his heart grew oddly warm as he neared the white stag. Sensing Moonstone's determined will matched his own, Derek braced as the great horse leaped up to mount the table as well.

The deer, still frozen, was closer than ever, perhaps worn down by the long pursuit. Now it leapt again; off the table and dashed toward the forest wall. But no! It tumbled. It rolled, trapped in the heavy vines which snaked out across the ground from the bottom of the table.

Derek halted Moonstone some dozen feet from the captive animal which breathed in shuddering snorts. The prince slid off the saddle and gripped his dagger from his belt. Moving toward the stag, he marked its steady gaze; its dark eye mirroring his movement. It waited, tense as a drawn bowstring. Derek held his hunter's knife but did not know his mind. Was this why he had chased the stag for so many hours? Would it not be lost the very moment he had taken his trophy? Then he felt it again; the heat beside his heart, but now it was hot, scalding. The tooth the Duchess had given him! He slipped it free of his shirt and held it out in his hand. It glowed a bright yellow, lighting his fingers in the dark. He turned to stare at the moon. A winged shape flapped across its yellow disk. Gorackle.

***

Max

Max was sure he had seen the long black neck of a sea serpent coming toward him in the inky water. Any second he knew the rows of sharp teeth would tear his little vessel. He would be lucky only to drown in the foul waters of Lake Doom. Still, he would not be taken like a frightened rabbit, he promised himself through clinched teeth. He was the son of Randrew and it would not do to die with his eyes closed. Wishing only that Jippit were at his side, he clasped his sword hilt in both hands and sprang to his feet shouting a hoarse battle cry.

Nothing happened. Instead of the wild fury of an angry sea serpent, he was met with only the stony quiet of the witch's tower. It stood tall above him, a dark finger poking through the mist, its tip invisible in the fog. Now this was certainly a frightening sight, but not nearly so bad as a sea monster. Max was almost happy as the punt bumped into the shore of the rocky island. Climbing out, he pulled his craft onto the rocks before he took a step toward the tower. He wanted to be certain he would have a way to leave this place.

When he had carefully finished securing the boat, he turned to face the tower. He walked, keeping his eyes on the windows high above for any sign of life. There was none, and for the first time Max began to feel a strange tingling of his neck. Perhaps what waited behind those empty windows was not alive? He felt the fear trying to slip into him and he began to hum a tune to keep his mind off it. His humming sounded ghastly here, so soft and low it made him think of a funeral march. He quit.

The clouds pulled away from the top of the tower. His heart jumped and he stopped in his tracks. Max now saw a single lighted window just beneath the pointed steeple. Could the witch be back? Fletcher had given no warning, but could anyone hope to know the traps of this powerful sorceress? A small voice seemed to speak to Max so easily that he almost obeyed it without thinking. "*Go back,*" it seemed to whisper, "*go back and tell Jippit you could not find the island. He doesn't ever have to know. None of them ever have to know.*" But as he turned back to face the boat, he remembered Jippit rising at the shepherd's table and calling Max his king. "If I turn back here, I am no king, but a coward and a liar, as well," he said to himself. "No, Jippit, not worthy to be a king, and not worthy to be your friend." With this he bit his lip and went on to the great metal doors of the tower.

Above the arch of the doors, written in scrolled letters, Max read: "*Who Enters Here Shall Perish of Fear — I Follow, Soon to Swallow.*" It was written in the old style and Max had trouble reading it but took its meaning quickly enough. He fought off a shudder and looked at the doors. Two large iron rings were hung from them with a carving of a cruel imp set inside each loop. Max touched the faces just to know that they were only carvings and then tried one of the rings. Much to his surprise and dread the door opened easily. The darkness beyond the doorway seemed to be waiting for him. He looked up at the words, "*Soon to Swallow,*" and tip-toed into the dark.

Inside it was so dark that Max could not see his hand before his face. He spread his arms in front of him and slid his feet across the cold stone floor. Almost at once he bumped into a wall and began to feel his way along it. Then his hand struck something braced against the masonry and he was glad to find it was an unlighted torch. He pulled his coat open and fumbled in his pouch for his small tinder box. He sat on the floor against the wall with the torch resting across his lap and struck his flint against the floor. He was afraid the shavings were too wet to catch the spark when a small flash of light sizzled to life. He held the glowing ember under the torch head, blowing on it until it caught and grew to a fine flame.

The room was full of the flickering light now and the shadows bobbed in all directions as Max stood and held up his torch. There was a small table and a chair in the center of the chamber, but otherwise it was empty. His eye caught the stairs that ran up the side of the wall and disappeared overhead. With his sword in one hand and torch in the other, Max started the long climb. He glanced back as he started up the wide stone steps. The room below was returning to darkness. He thought he heard something.

Now the stairs were narrowing, and he felt as if he were walking up a stone tunnel. He could see the steps just above him and the walls on either side. With each step they seemed to be closing in so that he could see very little other than the steps he was climbing. He turned again to listen. What was that strange sound? The words above the door came back, "*I follow...*" What followed, he wondered? There was only silence. He began to climb again.

As he climbed, Max began to remember things, dreams long forgotten. He tried to think of something else, anything else. He wished Jippit was there, or Fanzig. Then his thoughts stopped. What was that? He was certain he heard footsteps below him on the stairs. He turned and looked as hard as he could, but there was nothing; nothing but the dark beyond the torchlight. He waited in the silence for a long moment and then began to climb once more. He was listening closely now, and he was sure he heard it this time. Footsteps, louder footsteps, drawing nearer. He drew his sword and whirled around to meet . . . nothing. Quiet again. He took each step carefully now, straining for any sound. Yes, he heard it, over his own heartbeat, step for step, just following his own. It must be very near, he thought. He wanted to turn and look but fought against it. "It is nothing," he whispered. "I am just nervous." Max stared straight ahead as he climbed, not even glancing at the walls beside him. The footsteps mocked each of his own, growing louder and louder.

Max began to sweat, and his hands trembled as he pressed on. He was climbing past doorways. Pitch black openings. The nightmares pressed in on him from every side. Still he kept his eyes straight ahead and kept climbing. The steps behind him were booming now and he could stand it no longer. He began to run. The crashing roar following was almost upon him. Max was twisting to jump into one of the dark rooms when he tripped on the bulky shepherd's coat and tumbled down several steps. His sword clattered loudly down the stairs and he crouched in horror against the wall waiting for the awful thing to leap upon him. Again, there came the maddening silence and nothing, nothing on the stairs. Was he going mad? Max took a deep breath and leaned down to grasp his sword but was so nervous that it slipped from his fingers and dropped again. As the hilt hit the first step there was a loud boom. Max jerked his head in shock as a ringing clap followed every sliding bounce of the sword on the stairs. Finally, the booming died away and there was silence again. The prince sat there, amazed at what he had seen and heard. He slammed his fist against the step. A loud boom rocked up from below a moment later. He stood up slowly then jumped up and down. The roar was so loud he had to cover his ears. The stairs were hollow. They were made to shape an echo that followed the climber and grew louder with every step of the way.

Max swallowed with relief as he remembered the door's warning. "Who enters here, shall perish of fear — I follow, soon to swallow." He nodded. Yes, of course, your *fears* followed you on these terrible stairs, and had almost swallowed him. But perish? He wondered at that and then he remembered something. He went to the door he had been trying to reach when he had fallen, and peered in. His mouth dropped open as he understood the full meaning of the warning. The door did not lead to a room at all but opened out to the night sky. An open window. Had he entered he would have been dashed to pieces on the rocks below. Anger swelled up in Max as he wondered how many brave knights had tumbled to their doom. He picked up his sword and resumed his climb. He did not mind the wild booming now. Let whatever lay ahead know that a prince of Gaspaar was approaching. Let his echo be a drumming march, for he no longer would sneak timidly forward to face evil. He would let his flag fly now. The hair on Max's neck prickled as he marched. He would hold onto his lesson and try to face his fears from this time on, and fear nothing which had no face.

He came to the end of the stairs and could see the door to the high room of the tower. A small line of yellow light shown beneath the door. Max set the torch in a rack, tightened his grip on his sword and pushed the door open.

CHAPTER 28

THE BROKEN SPELLS

The room was lit by large golden candle-stands and Max could see that it was richly furnished in tapestries of unusual patterns. He braced himself and stepped onto the carpeted floor. A sharp voice met his entrance that froze his breath in his throat.

"*Who* are *you? If* I might ask?"

Max spun, raising his sword and setting his teeth for what waited. Instead of the Duchess, he found a girl about his age with jet black hair hanging in long tresses and crowned with a circlet of gold. She stood beside a covered dinner table set with an evening meal. She was a little taller than Max and wore a courtly yellow dress with a green cape. Though the girl seemed poised and unafraid, Max could see the reflection of a sharp bread knife she held behind her on the surface of a polished copper urn.

"Who *are* you?" she asked again.

Max looked around the room. He was not going to fall for another of the witch's tricks. He turned back to the girl. "Who are *you*?" he asked. "For all I know, you are an ogre in disguise or even the witch herself."

The girl frowned and her nose went up just a bit. "You are certainly no knight in armor, that's plain enough. I had expected Sir Drindil or at least Sir Whit. But I suppose you will have to do. I am the Princess Rhena, daughter of King Lull of Leorna! You may bow."

She was certainly stuffy enough to be a princess, Max thought. "Well," he answered, "I happen to be *the* Prince Max, son of Randrew, King of Gaspaar. So, you can forget that bow, Princess Rhena — and I would very much appreciate it if you would also set down that knife you hold behind you."

The princess brought the bread knife around before her with a frown and set the blade on the plate. "Why should I *believe* you are a prince?" the girl said, her face reddening. "You are dressed like a common peasant and you haven't bathed in a while either." She put her fingers to her nose in mockery.

Max's hands were on his hips. "Peasant or not, you had better be glad I have come. Those other knights of yours do not seem to have arrived."

Princess Rhena bit her lip. "Perhaps they have perished fighting some dragon trying to rescue me."

Max laughed. "Maybe they just haven't gotten around to searching for you yet. Not many knights in Lull's court would venture up Tarrand-Kitil if my brother Derek knows anything about them."

The girl was upset now. "Well, how did you learn of my capture, if not from Sir Drindil, or one of the other knights?"

Max put his sword in his belt. "I didn't know you *were* captured or imprisoned by anyone. I came here to take the witch's treasure."

Rhena folded her arms and sat down. She was shaking. "Well, you just go on then. Take your silly treasure and go. I'm not stopping you! Sir Drindil will be here soon, you'll see. The knights of my father's court would never abandon their princess."

Max saw he had hurt the girl's feelings. He looked around the small room and realized he had been afraid of the witch's return to this evil place from the moment he had left the punt. How terrifying to be her very *prisoner* here, like the princess, always subject to the sorceress' will? He swallowed. "Princess, I am sorry I have spoken rudely to you. It must be terrible to be shut up here with the witch herself and not able to get away. How long have you been here?"

The girl had closed her eyes and been taking breaths to calm herself. She opened her eyes and turned to look at Max. "I have been here for most of three weeks. Alone almost always, but she comes and goes as she wishes, as sudden as an evil laugh. She mocks me when she pays me any mind at all."

Max shuddered. "And you cannot leave this island tower for the foul evil water surrounding it. What does she say of her plans for you? How came she to capture you?"

Princess Rhena flashed a tiny smile and rubbed her eyes with her sleeve. "I was taken while exploring outside my castle's walls. I like to slip away from time to time. I *do* get so tired of being closed in, even in our palace." She sighed. "How I would like to be back in my father's castle *now*." Rhena paused a moment before she continued her story. She looked toward the door as she spoke, almost as if she were picturing it all again in her mind's eye. "She took me on the saddle of the nightmare horse she calls up with terrible words and signs. It was like a horrible dream, but I knew I must *not* show fear for her. Never! She *loves* fear."

Rhena turned to look at Max. "There is deep evil behind her beautiful face. She can speak with such . . . softness, kindness; but her words are tools to get inside your thoughts. To speak with her is to be confused and fooled, so I have spoken nothing since the second night of my imprisonment." She paused and added, "Only now, here with you . . . and alone in my prayers."

Max studied the girl. Truly she *was* brave; likely braver than he. He nodded. "I also have heard her soothing words and voice. My mind was swayed as well. Certainly, she must mean to ransom you from King Lull at some evil bargain. No doubt your father has sent brave knights to hunt for you as you say. This is a long way from Leorna. Such a search would be hard for knights of any court, so you must not think less of them for my angry words."

Rhena smiled wider and nodded. "I was angry too. And maybe a little afraid still. You must be a very brave prince to have come so far alone and faced her tower. She bragged that many bold knights have died trying to take it."

Max thought of the disguised doors on the stairs that concealed such deadly traps and was about to reply when he saw the chest.

It was a large black oaken box with dull brass bracing and a heavy iron lock. It sat on the floor beneath the glassed window Max had seen from below. He went to it and slowly bent down to study the latch, wondering if this was indeed the treasure he had ascended Tarrand Kitil to claim. Was this final metal guard the last restraint or was there yet another spell hidden, waiting for his touch? He took a breath and grabbed the latch. The lock was solid of course, but he felt no fierce bite of magic or sting of serpent's poison.

"How shall you open it without a key?" The princess asked, on her knees beside him now, staring at the forbidding lock.

Max nodded. "My mother once told me a tale of Alexander and a great knot he must unravel to open his way to Persia." He drew his sword. "I shall use the same key." He did not pause for an instant. Taking his sword in both hands he hacked at the wood around the metal. Muscles that had toughened with days of climbing swung the blade harder and harder as the oak splinters flew. The lock fell off the chest with a clunk and Max paused only an instant before he pushed back the lid.

"*Jewels,*" the princess whispered loudly. She turned to smile at Max. "I have never seen anything like them."

The boy and the girl sank down beside the open chest and ran their arms up to their elbows in the rich treasure. Emeralds, diamonds, rubies. Max had never imagined how beautiful they could be. They would pick up a trinket of gold-set emeralds only to drop it for a topaz-studded chalice or a diamond tiara. There were golden rings and silver rings, strings of pearls and sapphires. And there was the crown. A tall golden crown set with giant opals where a rainbow of colors danced in polished brilliance. The crown was lined with finest velvet and strange dwarf runes were cut in the golden band. Max raised it gently, staring at its majesty.

"Some dwarf king's treasure from long ago," he said. "Never has there been such a crown in Gaspaar."

The princess nodded and touched the crown with a nervous finger.

Max set it in the chest and turned to Rhena. "I am sorry I was mean to you, Princess Rhena. Please, forgive me. I have come a very long and hard way to find this. Come with me now and escape the witch."

Rhena looked down. "I should not have been so quick to mock you, Prince Max. We should be friends, I think." Then she laughed. "What a trick for the witch to find me *and* the treasure gone."

They shook hands and then, working together, began to drag the chest across the floor. It was very heavy, and Max dreaded going down the stairs. Suddenly he stood up and struck his hands to his head, crying out.

Rhena glanced up. "What is the matter, Prince Max? Have you hurt yourself?"

"No, no, no," Max moaned. "I had forgotten! Princess Rhena, do you not know that once anything has been taken from this tower against the witch's desire that it will sink into the lake?"

"Yes," Rhena said worriedly. "She told me of the spell and warned me not to try to escape while she was away. But with your boat we shall be safe, won't we?"

Max sat down on the chest and put his head in his hands. "Princess, my boat is very small. There is just room enough for you and me. There is no room for the treasure."

The princess was quiet and sat down beside Max. She put a hand on his shoulder.

Max tried not to cry but it just seemed so unfair. At last he had the treasure, and now everything was ruined.

Rhena finally spoke. "You . . . you came for the treasure, Prince Max. It . . . *it* is your destiny." She closed her eyes and swallowed before she whispered. "There is room enough for you and *it*."

Max looked up at the girl. He could hardly believe the words she had spoken. She was indeed a princess to say such a thing, but it was wrong. "No," he answered. "I could *never* be a king and do such a wretched thing. I have gone the wrong way at many turnings, but here there *is* no other way." He grinned weakly. "A knight follows his rules wherever he goes. If I break them now, being king would be worth nothing."

They were both quiet for a time, but Max finally got up and held his hand out for the princess. "Don't be afraid of the stairs," he said. "There is nothing to fear there. The loud steps are only our own echoes."

Rhena opened the trunk one last time and looked in. "At least take the crown, Max," she said.

He shook his head. "Only a rightful king should wear a crown. I am king of nothing."

Rhena reached down and took a large golden ring with a beautiful rune carved on it and placed it on Max's forefinger. "Now you may show others you were here."

Max swallowed and nodded. He then reached into the chest for the last time and lifted a simple silver chain with a small clear crystal pendant from the glorious depths within. "So, you can remember," he said, holding it up to Rhena and trying to smile. They began down the stairs with the booming echoes rolling below them like senseless laughter mocking their retreat.

When they finally came to the boat Max looked back up at the tower. "At least *she* will not have the treasure," he cried.

"Or her tower," Rhena added.

They climbed into the craft and Max shoved them away with the paddle. He kept paddling as hard as he could. Behind them the water started bubbling fiercely, then foaming, and now they could hear a grumbling bellow as if the mountain itself were angry. At that moment Max heard a terrible piercing shriek high in the air above them. He had heard it once before in the forest at the base of the mountain. There was no doubt of what it was. He turned to see Rhena pointing beyond the breaking mists. Her face was stricken.

"The *nightmare*! The witch comes!"

Max felt his heart fill with fire as he turned, his hand now reaching for his scabbard, though he doubted a sword alone could deny the attack of the sorceress astride her terrible mount. Then he remembered that fear was a power she cast against them, demanding their defeat. His pulse drummed in his head, but he saw nothing beyond the roiling steam. Then the punt began to rock, and he gripped the sides and bent low to steady the craft as waves rose about them.

Behind them Max heard the rising rumble of the island breaking up in the violent water of the lake. He glanced over his shoulder to see the tower shaking and stones falling from its heights. There was a sudden deafening roar as steam gushed past them hiding everything from their eyes.

Shouting encouragement to each other they braced themselves against whatever must next come. There was a great crashing splash behind, and they were drenched with a spray of hot water. The sound ended and the last waves fell. There was only silence. There was no nightmare screech and no sign of the witch. Max and Rhena stared about them. The tower was gone and everything in it.

***

Derek

Prince Derek let the tooth drop against his shirt and, seizing his dagger, moved to the stag. Its great eye glowed golden in the light of the tooth. With a sudden move, Derek gripped the twisted vines which bound the deer tight against the ground and slashed them through, freeing its powerful hooves. Though he expected no show of thanks for his rescue, Derek was still surprised at the response. The wild creature sprung upwards and whipping its head with a powerful lunge, struck out at the man standing over it. The head butted against his side, throwing him off balance. An antler point caught the lanyard that held the glowing dragon's tooth, ripping it loose and hurling it away in the brush. As he fell against the ground, Derek saw the stag rushing into the trees and Moonstone galloping after it, but his attention was jarred now elsewhere. The dragon had arrived.

The air split with the shriek of Gorackle and the wide batwings spread, blocking out a hundred stars. Green flame shot overhead as the evil lizard landed atop the flat table, claws clacking loudly on the stone. The blaze had licked out across the clearing at the departure of the stag and fiery pools of green flame marked a path where it had run. Derek, without his shield or helmet, was glad he had fallen into the tangle of brush and out of the dragon's sight for the moment. He had no need of the tooth the Duchess had given, for it was no longer a matter of hunting the dragon; instead, it seemed the dragon was hunting him. Certainly, the Gorackle hunted something. It turned its horned head slowly about in a wide sweep. He prayed that Moonstone would remain hidden, for if the steed ran to his protection, it would be burned or ripped by the dragon's claws.

Derek knew he could never outrun this creature, and with no shield to ward off flames, or lance to reach the towering head, he held little chance of survival. The only place he could see that afforded a moment's safety was the dark gap beneath the table. If only he could reach that place unseen. Then he saw the dragon blow fire into the air and the clearing was bright again for a moment, and then the queerest thing of all; the beast swung its head sharply to stare into the brush off to Derek's right, the beak bending down as the neck arched for a closer look into the undergrowth.

And there he saw what must surely have caught the monster's eye; a bright glowing light down in the bracken. He knew that light for it had glowed as it burned against his skin. It was the dragon's tooth. As the green eyes turned away from him, Derek rolled under the table edge. Just above him on the stone, rested the soft underbelly of the dragon. Slowly, quietly, he slid his sword from its scabbard.

CHAPTER 29

THE RETURN BEGINS

Max helped Rhena from the punt as soon as they scraped against the rocks and looked with question for any sign of the witch in the night sky. They had imagined the terrible winged horse set to swoop onto them with its evil mistress casting a horrible spell, but only silence and the starry sky met their stares. Rhena shook her head with wonder. Max sighed with relief as the tension uncoiled in his chest.

The princess sat down against a flat boulder. "Perhaps we imagined the scream. Perhaps her spells *themselves* scream when they are broken . . ." She looked to Max. "Did you actually see her?"

Uncertain, Max looked across the rim of the lake as the mists began to clear away. He shook his head. "I could not be sure. Now, everything is gone." He heard Jippit shouting in the distance and saw the elf scrambling around the curve of the stone beach toward them. He was slowed by the stumbling, grumbling, bound dwarf he led.

"Max! Max! You did it! By the Wizard's Beard, you *did* it!" Jippit was hollering as he hurried nearer.

"Not so fast, blast you!" Scrugnit complained as he was tugged along.

Max reached down to the rough shore and picked up a small stone to chunk against the water, skipping it over the black lake. He hardly knew what to say to the elf.

Jippit bounded up to them and grabbed Max by the arm. "Where is the treasure, Max? I heard the wicked tower crack and sink!" At that moment he recognized Max's silence and turning his head saw the princess sitting against the boulder for the first time.

"Princess *Rhena*? How . . . what . . .?" The elf stuttered in surprise.

"Jester Jippit?" Rhena was equally shocked to see the former jester. "What are you doing here?"

Max spoke softly. "She was a prisoner of the witch."

Jippit looked back to Max.

Max continued, turning away from the elf. "Jippit . . . I could not take the treasure."

The elf opened his mouth to speak but saw how sad Max was and did not.

Rhena stood and moved to Jippit's side. "Good elf," she

began, "Prince Max has saved my life. He has forsaken his great treasure to rescue me. Do not blame him. It is my fault."

Jippit looked over his shoulder to the girl and nodded. "I do not blame *anyone*, Princess, but he lost more than a treasure. He has lost a *kingdom* as well." Jippit turned away from them both and walked down the shore, kicking stones and muttering Elvish beneath his breath.

Rhena turned to Max who was looking after the elf. "Is he now *your* servant?" she asked.

"My *friend*," Max answered. Suddenly he turned around to look about them. "*Scrugnit!* Where is Scrugnit?" With that he began to run after Jippit.

Alone, Rhena felt suddenly tired and tears of relief came to her eyes. She fought a sob that seemed to be welling up in her throat when a kind voice spoke from behind her.

"There, there, young Princess. *I* should not be so sad at having escaped the Witch of the Runruggel Mountains."

Rhena gasped in amazement as a great owl lit on a rock beside her.

The feather-horned head tilted slightly. "When a true good thing is done, other good will come of it. Max and the elf may feel badly now. Feelings we do not control, but they cannot see the future." Fletcher's golden eyes blinked brilliant in the moonlight.

Rhena found words despite her amazement as she addressed the strange creature. "I would believe *anything* tonight. Tell me, Sir Owl — do *you* see into the future?"

Fletcher chuckled. "Great Izmah, no. But I do know how today flows out of yesterday and how tomorrow will flow from today. There are many, many sides to every moment, Princess. These two see only a dark side, but it is not the only side. Not nearly. Come with me now."

Rhena followed, amazed as the owl skittered over the

rocks in short glides toward the boy and the elf. She was almost freezing in the cold air, she realized; the warmer mists of the lake were near vanished now.

"Fletcher!" Max called out. "There is much, much to tell."

"Yes — of course," the owl answered. "But not now, there are *other* things for now. For one, the princess is freezing."

Rhena came up to them as the owl spoke and Max, chastened, slipped off his warm coat and helped her into the bulgy-fitting garment as Rhena thanked him. He pulled his sleeping blanket from his pack and drew it around his own shoulders.

"You have lost a treasure, Max," Fletcher was saying, "but you have brought much good this night. Look toward the cliffs."

Max and Jippit strained to see. "It is someone hobbling over the rocks," Max said with surprise, "but I cannot tell anything else."

Jippit was going to say something, but Fletcher spoke.

"*Ah*, I have forgotten your eyes, my boy," the owl blinked. "It is none other than the Witch of the Runruggle Mountains herself. She was flying here on her nightmare when her spells were broken by you and the princess. A nasty tumble she took. Rather mussed up, I'm afraid. No, she is still far too strong to conquer right now. You are not ready to face her . . . *neither* of you." The owl turned his head to Rhena. "Yet you have cut deeply into her power. Many will sleep better for your daring. It should be a time before she threatens this land again."

"There goes her pawn, Scrugnit, scrambling to her now," Jippit laughed bitterly. "Well, they deserve each other."

"And —" Fletcher continued, "you have saved the *life*

of a princess, young Max. Is that a deed to sulk at having done?"

The owl was scolding now, Max knew. He grinned and shook his head. He glanced at Rhena. "I forget myself, old Fletcher, with dreams of being king. I can't see the nose on my face. I have had a greater adventure than any brave knight would hope for." He laughed. "Just wait until the queen's maid back home hears of it!"

The climb down the mountain was difficult, but Max was surprised at how quickly the princess learned. *Not really a bad sort, for a girl*, he thought. She never complained with the bumps and scrapes. Strong too. He would not care to race her on even ground.

When at long last they stepped down off the rocky face of Tarrand-Kitil into the little clearing, Max saw that Knipper, Fanzig, and Blueberry were waiting for them. Fletcher had told them of all that had happened. They did not speak of it. Jippit took his great-grandfather's ring from the rocks and they began the long hike to Dimbarrel's farm. Max was glad to be on Blueberry once again and she didn't seem to mind carrying the princess as well.

"Dimbarrel's nephew Neale is watching the farm now, Max," Knipper said as they journeyed. "I shall return with you to the palace, if I may."

"And I," Fanzig said.

"And I," Jippit said.

"And I," Princess Rhena said.

"Well, yes — that is, yes — and I," Fletcher said.

Jippit cooked a splendid supper for them all when they at last arrived at the farm. Neale, the shepherd's nephew, was amazed at the odd company around the rough table.

"Elves and princesses and talking animals and bless my soul, if old Knipper isn't talking his self." Neale grinned. "Begging your pardon, Prince Max, but I think your horse and I are the only ones here not just a bit — *touched*."

They all laughed at that and Knipper told the boy that he was going on to the inn to see Dimbarrel and then to the palace with Max.

"Well," Neale stammered, "I always said you had a mind of your own, old Knipper. I just didn't guess you ever spoke it."

***

Gerald

The bucket rode upwards in the narrow round channel. Gerald stood with his feet set inside it and his hand gripping the tight rope. The handle above was turning, though no visible hand moved upon it. The prince watched the circle of stars overhead grow wider as he neared the top. He emerged into the full moonlight and climbed over the stone walls of the well. As he stood on the bare earth, he turned back to look down the way he had come. The cistern was now blocked, filled up with the same dry dust as the path he stood on. The creaky winding rod and frayed rope spoke of the well's long useless state. The lady had said that when one left the chamber of the green fire, that way was shut beyond might or spell. He would not return this way again. He smiled, remembering his entry so many underground days before. The prince had been a different person then; hungry and uncertain, but eager to learn, eager to know — to control.

Now he began his journey back to the court of his father. He held no chest of gold nor wore a ring of wealth or power, but he was carrying a treasure of different measure.

For Gerald now saw the world in a changed manner. The vision of mere men was limited to the ways they imagined the world ought to work. Their laws and customs were made to safeguard their petty courts and castles. He had learned much and wished to learn more, and the lady had promised that there would be time enough for that, if he should show wisdom in the use of his new craft. He knew well the first spell he would use in the courtyard of the king.

He was disappointed the Duchess had not come back from her errand to see him away. Neither had Lord Gorna returned from his journey north, though Gerald had not missed his prescribed mentor. In their absence the remaining council members seemed uncertain of Gerald's status. He had removed their resistance to his leaving when he showed them the tattoos that the lady had worked upon the palms of his hands. Visible only by the light of the green fire or moonlight, he lifted his palm now as the moon rode above him in the sky. It was there. The green eye, glowing with the power of the hidden vision. He whistled and soon Gonrest appeared on the ridge of the hill moving slowly toward him. The horse seemed anxious, uncertain. Gerald used a word of command and held the eye before him. Immediately the steed trotted toward him, faster and faster. It reared up in a wild pawing stance, as if to strike out with its hooves. At a sudden twist of Gerald's hand, the stallion settled down and knelt, crouching low, allowing him to mount by merely stepping across its saddle. For now, simple beasts obeyed his command, but the day would come when his skills were greater. Perhaps then, even humans might not resist his will. That day was not this one. Indeed, much he had learned would slide into his dreams to hide from his daylight mind, but all he had learned remained within, locked inside to wait where even he did not know.

***

Max

The long trip back to the inn on the Lumbadil was quite pleasant. There were no robbers on the road — none had been seen in weeks — and the weather was beautiful. They joked and sang most of the way. Everyone was trying to cheer Max's spirits.

By traveling on the main road, and without the sheep to slow their progress, they were making quite good time on their journey. It seemed that Max might just make it home on the last day of the month.

When they came to the Red Lion Inn at the river bridge, they were surprised to see so many travelers staying there. Joel and Maude recognized Max and made sure there was room. All the guests were on their way to the palace to see the test of the princes, the innkeeper told him, for word of the brothers' quest had gotten out. Then Maude led them to Dimbarrel's room.

The old shepherd was very glad to see them and bowed to both Max and Princess Rhena. Dimbarrel was much better now and wanted to know of all that had happened since he had been struck down with his fever.

That evening, Max, Jippit, Rhena and the shepherd ate together in the large dining room. They were not recognized as few beyond the palace had seen Max up close and certainly not dressed in such rough garb. The beasts didn't care for the crowd of strangers and stayed outside. Dimbarrel sat listening as Max told the whole tale. The shepherd would sometimes nod or shake his head in wonder as Max told him of the giant's cave, the dwarves' passage and the witch's tower.

When Max had finished, Dimbarrel stroked his white

beard. "There is little I can do to repay you for all you have done for me, young Prince. But I should like to go with you to your father's palace for the day of judgment if it is allowed. A man ought to have friends to stand by him in such a thing."

Max thanked the shepherd. As he sat eating his supper, he could overhear other guests trading rumors of the treasures his brothers were bringing back to the palace.

"Ahhh, that Derek. There never was a knight like that one," a fat man sighed putting down his tankard. "I hear he brings back tons of treasure in wagons of solid gold."

"That is nothing," his companion replied. "Gerald brings back power from under the mountains. They say he can throw a thunderbolt on a clear day by just clapping his hands!"

"What of Max?" another asked. "What do you hear of the youngest prince?"

The other two men looked at each other and shrugged. "Nothing . . ." they said.

"*They're right,*" Max thought sadly. "*Nothing.*"

CHAPTER 30

THE GREATEST TREASURE

The crowd was mumbling and murmuring as they waited for the signal trumpet. There was a good bit of pushing and shoving as more and more people tried to squeeze in. Everyone was pressing to get a better view of the royal courtyard. They had come from shops, farms, and stables to see, and they were going to have the best look they could get.

The three princes stood in a wide-open space surrounded on three sides by the crowd. There were guards to keep the square from being filled-in altogether.

Derek stood erect in his glistening armor, his hands resting on his hips and his polished broadsword at his side.

His brilliant red cloak fluttered easily in the morning breeze. Behind him, a large tent stood tall and mysterious, covered with beautiful designs and surrounded by guards. No one could get a peek inside.

Gerald posed tall in a long black robe of silk with white stars on the sleeves. He wore a green turban and bowed mockingly when Derek waved to him. Behind him was a small black tent of silk like his robe. A white dragon was painted on its sides and guards kept the curious from it also.

Max had entered the court at the last moment and had not even time to change his clothes. He waited nervously, his tattered green shirt stuffed into the remains of his britches. A few of the court noticed he was brown as a chestnut and his hair was longer and twisted from his days in the wild. He looked harder, too, the royal cook told his neighbor. A few noticed a large golden ring on his forefinger, but there was no tent behind him, just more crowd.

Finally, there was a blare of trumpets and the crowd cheered as King Randrew and Queen Maeve came down the steps of the palace to the courtyard; the king using his jeweled walking staff. When they reached the flat ground of the square, the crowd hushed.

Leaving the queen beside her royal chair, the king strode solemnly across the yard to stand before the three brothers. In a sudden breeze his purple robe flapped wildly behind him as he rested himself against his staff. Irritated with the noisy garment he slung it over his shoulder and tucked it into his sash. The crowd laughed and cheered. He smiled but raised a hand and everyone fell silent once again. Then he spoke.

"Loyal subjects of Gaspaar, you have heard the king grows old. The king is perhaps getting old enough to step down. Laugh as you will. I have heard this as well. Fortunately for our kingdom, I have three fine sons to take charge of the land when that day comes whenever it shall come. I have decided that I should none-the-less think of your future. I have set a great test to decide between my sons who shall reign when I hand down the crown."

The crowd went wild with applause and cheering. "That old buster will be glad to go to pasture sooner than he thinks," a fat merchant whispered in his wife's ear.

"Oh, hush," she replied. "His beard just turned gray early."

The merchant laughed and winked an eye, "but it's taking forever to turn white."

The king signaled for quiet again. "By now, most of you have heard that a month past I sent my sons into the wilds to bring back the greatest treasures they could find. I shall judge them by their treasures. I am certain that this shall not be easily done. I shall be as fair a judge as I have wit. The future of Gaspaar lies in the decision I shall make." The king's face was solemn as he studied each of his sons in silence.

Turning to his oldest son, he spoke. "Derek, what treasure have you brought?"

Derek grinned and clapped his hands. Two servants pulled ropes attached to the structure behind him and the tent fell away to reveal a hay wagon laden with gold coins. The body of a great scaly green dragon lay stretched across the treasure, its cold lifeless eyes were as big as dinner plates. The tips of its leathery wings drug on the ground.

The crowds gasped and drew back, then cheered wildly. "That's our Derek!" they cried. "What a *beast* — Look at the size of that monster — A fire-breather if ever I saw one — What a king Derek will make!"

Max grinned wide with pride at Derek's conquest. Always the hero, his oldest brother had not failed his expectations.

Derek held his arm out to the dragon. "This was Gorackle — the fiercest dragon I have ever met! His treasure weighs more than the worm himself. It is years of ransoms for princesses, and villages, cattle and farms, paid for terrible freedom from his fire and claws. A dozen knights have tried, none now ride, but I have slain Gorackle for *Gaspaar*."

The king smiled and nodded while the crowd cheered. Next, he walked to the place where Gerald stood. "And you, Gerald, what treasure have you?" he asked.

Gerald did not speak but bowed and walked into his tent. There was silence for a moment and then shouts of terror as a large dragon's head poked out of the entrance, its cruel jaw dropping, and a long black tongue curled outward in two wicked points.

The king stepped back as Derek rushed to his side. There was a cackling laugh and the dragon pranced out of the tent and whirred its wings sending dust clouds swirling upward in the courtyard. Derek grabbed his shield and held it before the king. Many of the crowd were pushing to get away while others pushed forward to see what had happened.

Stunned at this terrifying sight, Max grasped his sword and looked to his friends in the crowd. He saw Fanzig shake his head and Max wondered at the fox's calm. He waited nervously for what might follow but stood his ground.

There was a sudden flash of light and a haze of white smoke and Gerald stood where the dragon had been. He laughed.

"I bring you *power*, Father. The mysteries of the 'Wise Ones'. I found them and solved their riddles. Now I can appear as anything that walks upon the earth. No one may laugh at Gaspaar now. *This* I bring you."

There was much talk in the crowd now. Some were

glad to see such a display, but others were frightened. "With Gerald, we are safe from all our enemies!" a man shouted, and a muffled cheer went up.

The king looked at Gerald for a long time and then turned and taking up his staff walked to the place where Max waited. "What have *you* brought, my son?" he asked.

Max felt awful. He shifted his weight from one foot to the other. "Well, My Lord," he began, "Well, My Lord . . . I started out . . . I journeyed . . . there were things that had to be done on the way . . . the last chance . . . cost too much to keep." He took a deep breath. "I . . . guess I . . . have nothing." He swallowed, but the hard lump stayed in his throat. He could not look up.

There was quiet for a moment and then there was a titter — then a chuckle — and now some were starting to giggle. Others prodded the gigglers to be quiet, but the laughing had begun.

Everyone was surprised at a loud shout and in an instant the crowd was hushed. Jippit Jumpjilter was stamping red faced to stand beside Max.

"Your Majesty!" the elf cried. "Your Majesty, I am an elf and *no citizen* of Gaspaar, but it must be a land of *little* account if those as brave as young Max are laughed at for not bringing home pretty coins or parlor tricks. Your son saved my life again and again and if you throw me in prison for it now, I'll have my say."

The crowd was amazed at the angry little man. Many who had never seen an elf before began to laugh again in wonder and amusement.

A feebler voice rose and old Dimbarrel followed Jippit with his hat in his hands. Princess Rhena held his arm as he came forward. "Your Highness — I — I'm just a simple shepherd and I am not so bold as this good elf, but I owe your son all I have for saving my poor little flock I . . ." the rest of his words were lost in the excited commotion of the crowd as Knipper, Fanzig and Fletcher, padded, slunk and flew to Max's side.

Trying to be heard over the crowd, Knipper got so upset he started barking and Rhena fought the angry words that rose inside her and the tears on her face while Jippit got louder and redder. Fanzig was so busy trying to hide from some of the dogs among the throng that he was not speaking, and Fletcher couldn't seem to find the words he wanted. He kept starting over again with different royal greetings, "Your *Highness*, no — your *Majesty*, no— your *Grace* —" though he was not heard over the commotion.

King Randrew threw up his arm and everyone in the courtyard stopped laughing, talking, or even barking. The quiet was so strong you could almost hear it.

"Kneel," the king commanded.

Max dropped down on one knee and bowed his head. He wondered what words his father would have for all that had happened. Then he heard the king's clear voice again.

"My eldest son has brought back a great dragon's treasure with fierce strength and high courage. My second son has brought us a display of powerful mystical skill that few could imagine or acquire. Yet now, subjects of Gaspaar . . . I give you . . . your future *king*."

There was a great murmuring among the crowd and Max glanced up to see if he had heard his father's words correctly. The king was holding his own crown above Max's head. The young prince could say nothing. He couldn't even swallow. Then his father turned to the throng.

"My son has brought to us the treasure which strength beyond measure cannot win, which the greatest cleverness may never claim — the love of *true* friends." There was quiet as Randrew paused and then continued. "Kingdoms may fall from craft or power, but that which calls these to stand before us now, risking the king's anger though seeking no reward, has conquered this throne completely." He looked at the crown in his hands. "May Gaspaar *never* lose such treasure."

In the crowd the royal gardener turned to his wife. "The king's wisdom," he nodded with a smile.

"I never doubted it," the gardener's wife grinned back. "No matter what the wine steward said."

Near them the queen's maid smirked to the royal cook. "I knew it was to be Max all along!"

The cook looked back to the figure of the king holding his crown above the young prince's head. He smiled to himself. *You just never knew; the stables one day — the throne the next.*

There was a lot of cheering after this, though Max did not seem to hear it very well, and he could never remember much of the music and dancing. He only knew he was happy and tired and somehow, deep down inside, he felt a small sadness. Fanzig and Fletcher had disappeared in the celebration and as Dimbarrel and Knipper bid him farewell, he almost asked to go with them but only smiled and returned their goodbyes.

Derek gave Max a handshake and then a hug, laughing and telling Max he had begun to worry about being king anyway. He grinned, "A palace has four walls too many for me."

Gerald had bowed and congratulated him, but Max could see that his brother's pride was deeply hurt. There was a cold distance in his eyes that Max had not seen before. He would do everything he could to be a better brother to Gerald, he remembered promising at the shepherd's farm, and determined he would keep his promise.

King Randrew had called for a party of knights to be made ready to escort Princess Rhena to her father's court in Leorna. Now Sir Quinn and Sir Claire waited on their chargers along with the queen's own maid astride her noble mount. A fine mare stood groomed and saddled for the princess.

Princess Rhena turned to Max. "Now, Prince Max, it is time for me to bid you farewell. Despite our first meeting, I believe truly that your father has chosen well for a crown prince. You have courage and honor to equal any knight I have met. I pledge the friendship of my kingdom to live as long as my friendship to you. I will always remember your noble rescue from the tower of the witch, and its cost."

Max looked down, embarrassed at the princess' courtly words. "Princess, you know that I fought no combat to rescue you, and that there was no true choice to be made in giving up the treasure. I cannot pretend to be a hero."

Rhena nodded. "I know that, Max, and it is worth more than any shiny suit of armor or silver shield. Wear the golden ring from the witch's tower which I gave you. And sometimes, when you look upon it, remember our friendship as well as the treasure that you lost." Saying this, the princess leaned forward and kissed Max's cheek.

The prince flushed but grinned widely. "I have lost *nothing*," he said.

The princess walked to her waiting mount where an attendant squire lifted her to mount side-saddle. Rhena held a hand up to the applauding crowd and the small party of nobles turned and rode out of the courtyard.

After Princess Rhena had left for her father's court with the escort of Gaspaar's knights, Max found himself alone at last with Jippit Jumpjilter. He smiled at his friend. "I would never have gotten here without you, Jippit. You must be my council if I am to be crown prince. I am sorry to say that my adventures have probably ended now."

The elf looked back at Max in a knowing way and answered with narrowed eyes as he had often done by the campfire. "If you think you see clearly the way ahead of you, then you've learned little indeed among the wilds. Adventure chose you once, Max, and she has her hand upon you yet. Do not be surprised if your road does not end here."

Max began to grin and then to smile and finally he laughed, for once again he knew the elf was right.

THE END

Follow Max in the second tale of Gaspaar:

THE CLOUDS OF IZMAH

A passage from THE CLOUDS OF IZMAH

— Night air rushed against his face as Max strained for Jippit's directions above the howls rising behind. Scraping and scampering in a cold, black-blue world, fainter and fainter as the stars drifted out, the nightmare sounds were in his memory forever. Then a new sound, a crack, and an invisible force lifted Max from his seat and threw him bouncing and skidding on the hard dark ice. Max's tilting world spun to a stop and he found himself lying on his face.

For a moment he thought he might be dead. Then, hearing the wolves, the prince wondered if he were the only one still alive. He pulled himself to his knees and felt with relief that the tether on his wrist still held his sword. The elf's familiar voice was calling, and he shouted back as a new torch flickered to life on his left. The wolves' growls changed at this, and Max was aware of the wizard's tall shape standing above him.

"Come with me!" the wizard shouted. "Reen is hurt!"

Max scrambled after the light and felt Jippit's hand on his arm. He saw the elf held his sword as well. "The throat, Max. Don't go for the heart, it's too hard a kill," Jippit said evenly as he backed toward the overturned ice boat looking into the following dark.

Max looked down at the stricken figure of Reen who groaned in pain. "Is he dying?"

"Only if we do," the wizard replied. "The fire has made them cautious, but their blood is up. They'll be on us in a moment." —

Visit the author's website for information on the Max Series at the address below:

http://www.davidwwalkerwrites.com